Praise for Gayle Forman

if i stay

'This sensitively written story of the power of love and loss presses all
the right buttons . . . Read it, as they say, and weep'
Daily Mail

'Sometimes painful, other times funny but always touching, *If I Stay*
is a remarkably fresh and compelling piece of work. It's a book with
real heart, a book that makes you feel truly grateful to be alive'
Irish Independent

STARRED REVIEW – 'laced with insight, good humor, and wonder'
Booklist (US)

'A beautifully written book with moments of real sadness, hope,
laughter, tragedy and joy, which make you appreciate all the little
things you love, as your eyes brim with tears'
www.booktrust.org.uk

where she went

STARRED REVIEW – 'Forman follows up her bestselling *If I Stay*
with a story that is equally if not more powerful'
Publishers Weekly (US)

'Utterly breathtaking' *The Crooked Shelf*

'Forman writes in beautiful, elegant prose that is so saturated with
emotion it can't fail to give you the occasional lump in your throat'
Sugarscape

'A stunning sequel, beautifully written, with characters that will
capture your heart' *www.iwanttoreadthat.com*

www.**totallyrandombooks**.co.uk

Also available by Gayle Forman

Where She Went
Just One Day
Just One Year
Just One Night

Visit Gayle at
www.gayleforman.com

if i stay

GAYLE FORMAN

Definitions

IF I STAY

A DEFINITIONS BOOK 978 1 909 53123 9

First published in the United States by Dutton Children's Books, a member of
Penguin Group (USA) Inc.

Published in Great Britain by Definitions,
an imprint of Random House Children's Publishers UK
A Random House Group Company

This edition published 2014

7 9 10 8

The Random House Group Limited supports the Forest Stewardship Council® (FSC®),
the leading international forest-certification organisation. Our books carrying the FSC
label are printed on FSC®-certified paper. FSC is the only forest-certification scheme
supported by the leading environmental organisations, including Greenpeace. Our paper
procurement policy can be found at www.randomhouse.co.uk/environment

MIX
Paper from
responsible sources
FSC® C016897

Set in Berkeley by Falcon Oast Graphic Art Ltd

Definitions are published by Random House Children's Publishers UK,
61–63 Uxbridge Road, London W5 5SA

www.randomhousechildrens.co.uk
www.totallyrandombooks.co.uk
www.randomhouse.co.uk

Addresses for companies within The Random House Group Limited
can be found at: www.randomhouse.co.uk/offices.htm

THE RANDOM HOUSE GROUP Limited Reg. No. 954009

A CIP catalogue record for this book is available from the British Library.

Printed and bound by CPI Group (UK) Ltd, Croydon, CR0 4YY

FOR NICK

FINALLY . . . ALWAYS

7:09 a.m.

Everyone thinks it was because of the snow. And in a way, I suppose that's true.

I wake up this morning to a thin blanket of white covering our front lawn. It isn't even an inch, but in this part of Oregon a slight dusting brings everything to a standstill as the one snowplow in the county gets busy clearing the roads. It is wet water that drops from the sky – and drops and drops and drops – not the frozen kind.

It is enough snow to cancel school. My little brother, Teddy, lets out a war whoop when Mom's AM radio announces the closures. 'Snow day!' he bellows. 'Dad, let's go make a snowman.'

My dad smiles and taps on his pipe. He started smoking one recently as part of this whole 1950s, *Father Knows Best* retro kick he is on. He also wears bow ties. I am never quite clear on whether all this is sartorial or sardonic – Dad's way of announcing that he used to be a punker but is now a middle-school English teacher, or if becoming a teacher has actually turned my dad into this genuine throwback. But I like the smell of the pipe tobacco. It is sweet and smoky, and reminds me of winters and wood-stoves.

'You can make a valiant try,' Dad tells Teddy. 'But it's hardly sticking to the roads. Maybe you should consider a snow amoeba.'

I can tell Dad is happy. Barely an inch of snow means that all the schools in the county are closed, including my high school and the middle school where Dad works, so it's an unexpected day off for him, too. My mother, who works for a travel agent in town, clicks off the radio and pours herself a second cup of coffee. 'Well, if you lot are playing hooky today, no way I'm going to work. It's simply not right.' She picks up the telephone to call in. When she's done, she looks at us. 'Should I make breakfast?'

Dad and I guffaw at the same time. Mom makes cereal and toast. Dad's the cook in the family.

Pretending not to hear us, she reaches into the cabinet for a box of Bisquick. 'Please. How hard can it be? Who wants pancakes?'

'I do! I do!' Teddy yells. 'Can we have chocolate chips in them?'

'I don't see why not,' Mom replies.

'Woo-hoo!' Teddy yelps, waving his arms in the air.

'You have far too much energy for this early in the morning,' I tease. I turn to Mom. 'Maybe you shouldn't let Teddy drink so much coffee.'

'I've switched him to decaf,' Mom volleys back. 'He's just naturally exuberant.'

'As long as you're not switching *me* to decaf,' I say.

'That would be child abuse,' Dad says.

Mom hands me a steaming mug and the newspaper.

'There's a nice picture of your young man in there,' she says.

'Really? A picture?'

'Yep. It's about the most we've seen of him since summer,' Mom says, giving me a sidelong glance with her eyebrow arched, her version of a soul-searching stare.

'I know,' I say, and then without meaning to, I sigh. Adam's band, Shooting Star, is on an upward spiral, which is a great thing – mostly.

'Ah, fame, wasted on the youth,' Dad says, but he's smiling. I know he's excited for Adam. Proud even.

I leaf through the newspaper to the calendar section. There's a small blurb about Shooting Star, with an even smaller picture of the four of them, next to a big article about Bikini and a huge picture of the band's lead singer: punk-rock-diva Brooke Vega. The bit about them basically says that local band Shooting Star is opening for Bikini on the Portland leg of Bikini's national tour. It doesn't mention the even-bigger-to-me news that last night Shooting Star headlined at a club in Seattle and, according to the text Adam sent me at midnight, sold out the place.

'Are you going tonight?' Dad asks.

'I was planning to. It depends if they shut down the whole state on account of the snow.'

'It *is* approaching a blizzard,' Dad says, pointing to a single snowflake floating its way to the earth.

'I'm also supposed to rehearse with some pianist from the college that Professor Christie dug up.' Professor Christie, a retired music teacher at the university who I've been work-ing with for the last few years, is always looking for victims for me to play with. 'Keep you sharp so you can show all those Juilliard snobs how it's really done,' she says.

I haven't gotten into Juilliard yet, but my audition went really well. The Bach suite and the Shostakovich had both flown out of me like never before, like my fingers were just an extension of the strings and bow. When I'd finished play-ing, panting, my legs shaking from pressing together so hard, one judge had clapped a little, which I guess doesn't happen very often. As I'd shuffled out, that same judge had told me that: 'it had been a long time since the school had seen an Oregon country girl'. Professor Christie had taken that to mean a guaranteed acceptance. I wasn't so sure that

4

was true. And I wasn't 100 per cent sure that I wanted it to be true. Just like with Shooting Star's meteoric rise, my admission to Juilliard – if it happens – will create certain complications, or, more accurately, would compound the complications that have already cropped up in the last few months.

'I need more coffee. Anyone else?' Mom asks, hovering over me with the ancient percolator.

I sniff the coffee, the rich, black, oily French roast we all prefer. The smell alone perks me up. 'I'm pondering going back to bed,' I say. 'My cello's at school, so I can't even practice.'

'Not practice? For twenty-four hours? Be still, my broken heart,' Mom says. Though she has acquired a taste for classical music over the years – 'it's like learning to appreciate a stinky cheese' – she's been a not-always-delighted captive audience for many of my marathon rehearsals.

I hear a crash and a boom coming from upstairs. Teddy is pounding on his drum kit. It used to belong to Dad. Back when he'd played drums in a big-in-our-town, unknown-anywhere-else band, back when he'd worked at a record store.

Dad grins at Teddy's noise, and seeing that, I feel a familiar pang. I know it's silly but I have always wondered if Dad is disappointed that I didn't become a rock chick. I'd meant to. Then, in third grade, I'd wandered over to the cello in music class – it looked almost human to me. It looked like if you played it, it would tell you secrets, so I started playing. It's been almost ten years now and I haven't stopped.

'So much for going back to sleep,' Mom yells over Teddy's noise.

'What do you know, the snow's already melting.' Dad says, puffing on his pipe. I go to the back door and peek outside. A patch of sunlight has broken through the clouds, and I can hear the hiss of the ice melting. I close the door and go back to the table.

'I think the county overreacted,' I say.

'Maybe. But they can't un-cancel school. Horse is already out of the barn, and I already called in for the day off,' Mom says.

'Indeed. But we might take advantage of this unexpected boon and go somewhere,' Dad says. 'Take a drive. Visit Henry and Willow.' Henry and Willow are a couple of Mom and Dad's old music friends who'd also had a kid and decided to start behaving like grown-ups. They live in a big old farmhouse. Henry does Web stuff from the barn they converted into a home office and Willow works at a nearby hospital. They have a baby girl. That's the real reason Mom and Dad want to go out there. Teddy having just turned eight and me

6

being seventeen means that we are long past giving off that sour-milk smell that makes adults melt.

'We can stop at BookBarn on the way back,' Mom says, as if to entice me. BookBarn is a giant, dusty old used-book store. In the back they keep a stash of twenty-five-cent classical records that nobody ever seems to buy except me. I keep a pile of them hidden under my bed. A collection of classical records is not the kind of thing you advertise.

I've shown them to Adam, but that was only after we'd already been together for five months. I'd expected him to laugh. He's such the cool guy with his pegged jeans and black low-tops, his effortlessly beat-up punk-rock tees and his subtle tattoos. He is so not the kind of guy to end up with someone like me. Which was why when I'd first spotted him watching me at the music studios at school two years ago, I'd been convinced he was making fun of me and I'd hidden from him. Anyhow, he hadn't laughed. It turned out he had a dusty collection of punk-rock records under his bed.

'We can also stop by Gran and Gramps for an early dinner,' Dad says, already reaching for the phone. 'We'll have you back in plenty of time to get to Portland,' he adds as he dials.

'I'm in,' I say. It isn't the lure of BookBarn, or the fact that Adam is on tour, or that my best friend, Kim, is busy doing yearbook stuff. It isn't even that my cello is at school or that I could stay home and watch TV or sleep. I'd actually rather go off with my family. This is another thing you don't advertise about yourself, but Adam gets that, too.

'Teddy,' Dad calls. 'Get dressed. We're going on an adventure.'

Teddy finishes off his drum solo with a crash of cymbals. A moment later he's bounding into the kitchen fully dressed, as if he'd pulled on his clothes while careening down the steep wooden staircase of our drafty Victorian house. He started belting out the lines to 'School's Out'.

'Alice Cooper?' Dad asks. 'Have we no standards? At least sing the Ramones.'

Teddy carried on singing the tune over Dad's protests.

'Ever the optimist,' I say.

Mom laughs. She puts a plate of slightly charred pancakes down on the kitchen table. 'Eat up, family.'

8:17 a.m.

We pile into the car, a rusting Buick that was already old when Gran gave it to us after Teddy was born. Mom and Dad offer to let me drive, but I say no. Dad slips behind the wheel. He likes to drive now. He'd stubbornly refused to get

8

a license for years, insisting on riding his bike everywhere. Back when he played music, his unwillingness to drive meant that his bandmates were the ones stuck behind the wheel on tours. They used to roll their eyes at him. Mom had done more than that. She'd pestered, cajoled, and sometimes yelled at Dad to get a license, but he'd insisted that he preferred pedal power. 'Well, then you better get to work on building a bike that can hold a family of three and keep us dry when it rains,' she'd demanded. To which Dad always had laughed and said that he'd get on that.

But when Mom had gotten pregnant with Teddy, she'd put her foot down. Enough, she said. Dad seemed to understand that something had changed. He'd stopped arguing and had gotten a driver's license. He'd also gone back to school to get his teaching certificate. I guess it was OK to be in arrested development with one kid. But with two, time to grow up. Time to start wearing a bow tie.

He has one on this morning, along with a flecked sport coat and vintage wingtips. 'Dressed for the snow, I see,' I say.

'I'm like the post office,' Dad replies, scraping the snow off the car with one of Teddy's plastic dinosaurs that are scattered on the lawn. 'Neither sleet nor rain nor a half inch of snow will compel me to dress like a lumberjack.'

'Hey, my relatives were lumberjacks,' Mom warns. 'No making fun of the white-trash woodsmen.'

'Wouldn't dream of it,' Dad replies. 'Just making stylistic contrasts.'

Dad has to turn the ignition over a few times before the car chokes to life. As usual, there is a battle for stereo dominance. Mom wants the news. Dad wants Frank Sinatra. Teddy wants SpongeBob SquarePants. I want the classical-music station, but recognizing that I'm the only classical fan in the family, I am willing to compromise with Shooting Star.

Dad brokers the deal. 'Seeing as we're missing school today, we ought to listen to the news for a while so we don't become ignoramuses—'

'I believe that's ignoramusi,' Mom says.

Dad rolls his eyes and clasps his hand over Mom's and clears his throat in that schoolteachery way of his. 'As I was saying, the news first, and then when the news is over, the classical station. Teddy, we will not torture you with that. You can use the Discman,' Dad says, starting to disconnect the portable player he's rigged to the car radio. 'But you are not allowed to play to Alice Cooper in my car. I forbid it.' Dad reaches into the glove box to examine what's inside. 'How about Jonathan Richman?'

'I want SpongeBob. It's in the machine,' Teddy shouts, bouncing up and down and pointing to the Discman. The chocolate-chip pancakes dowsed in syrup have clearly only enhanced his hyper excitement.

'Son, you break my heart,' Dad jokes. Both Teddy and I were raised on the goofy tunes of Jonathan Richman, who is Mom and Dad's musical patron saint.

Once the musical selections have been made, we are off. The road has some patches of snow, but mostly it's just wet. But this is Oregon. The roads are always wet. Mom used to joke that it was when the road was dry that people ran into trouble. 'They get cocky, throw caution to the wind, drive like assholes. The cops have a field day doling out speeding tickets.'

I lean my head against the car window, watching the scenery zip by, a tableau of dark-green fir trees dotted with snow, wispy strands of white fog, and heavy gray storm clouds up above. It's so warm in the car that the windows keep fogging up, and I draw little squiggles in the condensation.

When the news is over, we turn to the classical station. I hear the first few bars of Beethoven's Cello Sonata no. 3, which was the very piece I was supposed to be working on this afternoon. It feels like some kind of cosmic coincidence. I concentrate on the notes, imagining myself playing, feeling grateful for this chance to practice, happy to be in a warm car with my sonata and my family. I close my eyes.

You wouldn't expect the radio to work afterward. But it does.

The car is eviscerated. The impact of a four-ton pickup truck going sixty miles an hour plowing straight into the passenger side had the force of an atom bomb. It tore off the doors, sent the front-side passenger seat through the driver's-side window. It flipped the chassis, bouncing it across the road and ripped the engine apart as if it were no stronger than a spider web. It tossed wheels and hubcaps deep into the forest. It ignited bits of the gas tank, so that now tiny flames lap at the wet road.

And there was so much noise. A symphony of grinding, a chorus of popping, an aria of exploding, and finally, the sad clapping of hard metal cutting into soft trees. Then it went quiet, except for this: Beethoven's Cello Sonata no. 3, still playing. The car radio somehow still is attached to a battery and so Beethoven is broadcasting into the once-again tranquil February morning.

At first I figure everything is fine. For one, I can still hear the Beethoven. Then there's the fact that I am standing here in a ditch on the side of the road. When I look down, the jean skirt, cardigan sweater, and the black boots I put on this morning all look the same as they did when we left the house.

I climb up the embankment to get a better look at the car. It isn't even a car anymore. It's a metal skeleton, without seats, without passengers. Which means the rest of my family must have been thrown from the car like me. I brush off my hands onto my skirt and walk into the road to find them.

I see Dad first. Even from several feet away, I can make out the protrusion of the pipe in his jacket pocket. 'Dad,' I call, but as I walk toward him, the pavement grows slick and there are gray chunks of what looks like cauliflower. I know what I'm seeing right away but it somehow does not immediately connect back to my father. What springs into my mind are those news reports about tornadoes or fires, how they'll ravage one house but leave the one next door intact. Pieces of my father's brain are on the asphalt. But his pipe is in his left breast pocket.

I find Mom next. There's almost no blood on her, but her lips are already blue and the whites of her eyes are completely red, like a ghoul from a low-budget monster movie. She seems totally unreal. And it is the sight of her looking like some preposterous zombie that sends a hummingbird of panic ricocheting through me.

I need to find Teddy! Where is he? I spin around, suddenly frantic, like the time I lost him for ten minutes at the grocery store. I'd been convinced he'd been kidnapped. Of course, it had turned out that he'd wandered over to inspect the candy aisle. When I found him, I hadn't been sure whether to hug him or yell at him.

I run back toward the ditch where I came from and I see a hand sticking out. 'Teddy! I'm right here!' I call. 'Reach up. I'll pull you out.' But when I get closer, I see the metal glint of a silver bracelet with tiny cello and guitar charms. Adam gave it to me for my seventeenth birthday. It's my bracelet. I was wearing it this morning. I look down at my wrist. I'm still wearing it now.

I edge closer and now I know that it's not Teddy lying there. It's me. The blood from my chest has seeped through my shirt, skirt and sweater, and is now pooling like paint drops on the virgin snow. One of my legs is askew, the skin and muscle peeled away so that I can see white streaks of bone. My eyes are closed, and my dark-brown hair is wet and rusty with blood.

I spin away. This isn't right. This cannot be happening. We are a family, going on a drive. This isn't real. I must have fallen asleep in the car. *No! Stop. Please stop. Please wake up!* I scream into the chilly air. It's cold. My breath should smoke. It doesn't. I stare down at my wrist, the one that looks fine, untouched by blood and gore, and I pinch as hard as I can.

I don't feel a thing.

I have had nightmares before – falling nightmares, playing- a-cello-recital-without-knowing-the-music nightmares, break-up-with-Adam nightmares – but I have always been able to command myself to open my eyes, to lift my head from the pillow, to halt the horror movie playing behind my closed lids. I try again. *Wake up!* I scream. *Wake up! Wakeupwakeupwakeup!* But I can't. I don't.

Then I hear something. It's the music. I can still hear the music. So I concentrate on that. I finger the notes of Beethoven's Cello Sonata no. 3 with my hands, as I often do when I listen to pieces I am working on. Adam calls it 'air cello.' He's always asking me if one day we can play a duet, him on air guitar, me on air cello. 'When we're done, we can thrash our air instruments,' he jokes. 'You know you want to.'

I play, just focusing on that, until the last bit of life in the car dies, and the music goes with it.

It isn't long after that the sirens come.

9:23 a.m.

Am I dead?

I actually have to ask myself this.

Am I dead?

At first it seemed obvious that I am. That the standing-here-watching part was temporary, an intermission before the bright light and the life-flashing-before-me business that would transport me to wherever I'm going next.

Except the paramedics are here now, along with the police and the fire department. Someone has put a sheet over my father. And a fireman is zipping Mom up into a plastic bag. I hear him discuss her with another firefighter, who looks like he can't be more than eighteen. The older one explains to the rookie that Mom was probably hit first and killed instantly, explaining the lack of blood. 'Immediate cardiac arrest,' he says. 'When your heart can't pump blood, you don't really bleed. You seep.'

I can't think about that, about Mom seeping. So instead I think how fitting it is that she was hit first, that she was the one to buffer us from the blow. It wasn't her choice, obviously, but it was her way.

But am I dead? The me who is lying on the edge of the road, my leg hanging down into the gulley, is surrounded by a team of men and women who are performing frantic ablutions over me and plugging my veins with I do not know what. I'm half naked, the paramedics having ripped open the top of my shirt. One of my breasts is exposed. Embarrassed, I look away.

The police have lit flares along the perimeter of the scene and are instructing cars in either direction to turn back, the road is closed. The police politely offer alternate routes, back roads that will take people where they need to be.

They must have places to go, the people in these cars, but a lot of them don't turn back. They climb out of their cars, hugging themselves against the cold. They appraise the scene. And then they look away, some of them crying, one woman throwing up into the ferns on the side of the road. And even though they don't know who we are or what has happened, they pray for us. I can feel them praying.

Which also makes me think I'm dead. That and the fact my body seems to be completely numb, though to look at me, at the leg that the sixty m.p.h. asphalt exfoliant has pared down to the bone, I should be in agony. And I'm not crying, either, even though I *know* that something unthinkable has just happened to my family. We are like Humpty Dumpty and all these king's horses and all these king's men cannot put us back together again.

I am pondering these things when the medic with the freckles and red hair who has been working on me answers my question. 'Her Glasgow Coma is an eight. Let's bag her now!' she screams.

She and the lantern-jawed medic snake a tube down my throat, attach a bag with a bulb to it, and start pumping. 'What's the ETA for Life Flight?'

'Ten minutes,' answers the medic. 'It takes twenty to get back to town.'

'We're going to get her there in fifteen if you have to speed like a fucking demon.'

I can tell what the guy is thinking. That it won't do me any good if they get into a crash, and I have to agree. But he doesn't say anything. Just clenches his jaw. They load me into the ambulance; the redhead climbs into the back with me. She pumps my bag with one hand, adjusts my IV and my monitors with the other. Then she smoothes a lock of hair from my forehead.

'You hang in there,' she tells me.

*

I played my first recital when I was ten. I'd been playing cello for two years at that point. At first, just at school, as part of the music program. It was a fluke that they even had a cello; they're very expensive and fragile. But some old literature professor from the university had died and bequeathed his Hamburg to our school. It mostly sat in the corner. Most kids wanted to learn to play guitar or saxophone.

When I announced to Mom and Dad that I was going to become a cellist, they both burst out laughing. They apologized about it later, claiming that the image of pint-size me with such a hulking instrument between my spindly legs had made them crack up. Once they'd realized I was

18

serious, they immediately swallowed their giggles and put on supportive faces.

But their reaction still stung – in ways that I never told them about, and in ways that I'm not sure they would've understood even if I had. Dad sometimes joked that the hospital where I was born must have accidentally swapped babies because I look nothing like the rest of my family. They are all blond and fair and I'm like their negative image, brown hair and dark eyes. But as I got older, Dad's hospital joke took on more meaning than I think he intended. Sometimes I did feel like I came from a different tribe. I was not like my outgoing, ironic dad or my tough-chick mom. And as if to seal the deal, instead of learning to play electric guitar, I'd gone and chosen the cello.

But in my family, playing music was still more important than the type of music you played, so when after a few months it became clear that my love for the cello was no passing crush, my parents rented me one so I could practice at home. Rusty scales and triads led to first attempts at 'Twinkle, Twinkle, Little Star' that eventually gave way to basic *études* until I was playing Bach suites. My middle school didn't have much of a music program, so Mom found me a private teacher, a college student who came over once a week. Over the years there was a revolving batch of students who taught me, and then, as my skills surpassed theirs, my student teachers played with me.

This continued until ninth grade, when Dad, who'd known Professor Christie from when he'd worked at the music store, asked if she might be willing to offer me private lessons. She agreed to listen to me play, not expecting much, but as a favor to Dad, she later told me. She and Dad listened downstairs while I was up in my room practicing a Vivaldi sonata. When I came down for dinner, she offered to take over my training.

My first recital, though, was years before I met her. It was at a hall in town, a place that usually showcased local bands, so the acoustics were terrible for unamplified classical. I was playing a cello solo from Tchaikovsky's 'Dance of the Sugar Plum Fairy'.

Standing backstage, listening to other kids play scratchy violin and clunky piano compositions, I'd almost chickened out. I'd run to the stage door and huddled on the stoop outside, hyperventilating into my hands. My student teacher had flown into a minor panic and had sent out a search party.

Dad found me. He was just starting his hipster-to-square transformation, so he was wearing a vintage suit, with a studded leather belt and black ankle boots.

'You OK, Mia Oh-My-Uh?' he asked, sitting down next to me on the steps.

I shook my head, too ashamed to talk.

'What's up?'

'I can't do it,' I cried.

Dad cocked one of his bushy eyebrows and stared at me with his gray-blue eyes. I felt like some mysterious foreign species he was observing and trying to figure out. He'd been playing in bands for ever. Obviously, he *never* got something as lame as stage fright.

'Well, that would be a shame,' Dad said. 'I've got a dandy of a recital present for you. Better than flowers.'

'Give it to someone else. I can't go out there. I'm not like you or Mom or even Teddy.' Teddy was just six months old at that point, but it was already clear that he had more personality, more verve, than I ever would. And of course, he was blond and blue-eyed. Even if he weren't, he'd been born in a birthing center, not a hospital, so there was no chance of an accidental baby swapping.

'It's true,' Dad mused. 'When Teddy gave his first harp concert, he was cool as cucumber. Such a prodigy.'

I laughed through my tears. Dad put a gentle arm around my shoulder. 'You know that I used to get the most ferocious jitters before a show.'

I looked at Dad, who always seemed absolutely sure of everything in the world. 'You're just saying that.'

He shook his head. 'No, I'm not. It was god-awful. And I

was the drummer, way in the back. No one even paid any attention to me.'

'So what did you do?' I asked.

'He got wasted,' Mom interjected, poking her head out the stage door. She was wearing a black vinyl miniskirt, a red tank top, and Teddy, droolingly happy from his BabyBjörn. 'A pair of forty-ouncers before the show. I don't recommend that for you.'

'Your mother is probably right,' Dad said. 'Social services frowns on drunk ten-year-olds. Besides, when I dropped my drumsticks and puked onstage, it was punk. If you drop your bow and smell like a brewery, it will look gauche. You classical-music people are so snobby that way.'

Now I was laughing. I was still scared, but it was somehow comforting to think that maybe stage fright was a trait I'd inherited from Dad; I wasn't just some foundling, after all.

'What if I mess it up? What if I'm terrible?'

'I've got news for you, Mia. There's going to be all kinds of terrible in there, so you won't really stand out,' Mom said. Teddy gave a squeal of agreement.

'But seriously, how do you get over the jitters?'

Dad was still smiling but I could tell he had turned serious because he slowed down his speech. 'You don't. You just work through it. You just hang in there.'

So I went on. I didn't blaze through the piece. I didn't achieve glory or get a standing ovation, but I didn't muck it up entirely, either. And after the recital, I got my present. It was sitting in the passenger seat of the car, looking as human as that cello I'd been drawn to two years earlier. It wasn't a rental. It was mine.

10:12 a.m.

When my ambulance gets to the nearest hospital – not the one in my hometown but a small local place that looks more like an old-age home than a medical center – the medics rush me inside. 'I think we've got a collapsed lung. Get a chest tube in her and move her out!' the nice red-haired medic screams as she passes me off to a team of nurses and doctors.

'Where's the rest?' asks a bearded guy in scrubs.

'Other driver suffering mild concussions, being treated at the scene. Parents DOA. Boy, approximately seven years old, just behind us.'

I let out a huge exhale, as though I've been holding my breath for the last twenty minutes. After seeing myself in that ditch, I had not been able to look for Teddy. If he were like Mom and Dad, like me, I . . . I didn't want to even think about it. But he isn't. He is alive.

23

They take me into a small room with bright lights. A doctor dabs some orange stuff onto the side of my chest and then rams a small plastic tube in me. Another doctor shines a flashlight into my eye. 'Non-responsive,' he tells the nurse. 'The chopper's here. Get her to Trauma. Now!'

They rush me out of the ER and into the elevator. I have to jog to keep up. Right before the doors close, I notice that Willow is here. Which is odd. We were meant to be visiting her and Henry and the baby at home. Did she get called in because of the snow? Because of us? She rushes around the hospital hall, her face a mask of concentration. I don't think she even knows it is us yet. Maybe she even tried to call, left a message on Mom's cell phone, apologizing that there'd been an emergency and she wouldn't be home for our visit.

The elevator opens right onto the roof. A helicopter, its blades swooshing the air, sits in the middle of a big red circle.

I've never been in a helicopter before. My best friend, Kim, has. She went on an aerial flight over Mount St Helens once with her uncle, a big-shot photographer for *National Geographic*.

'There he was, talking about the post-volcanic flora and I puked right on him and all over the cameras,' Kim told me in homeroom the next day. She still looked a little green from the experience.

Kim is on yearbook and has hopes of becoming a photographer. Her uncle had taken her on this trip as a favor, to nurture her budding talent. 'I even got some on his cameras,' Kim lamented. 'I'll never be a photographer now.'

'There are all kinds of different photographers,' I told her. 'You don't necessarily need to go flying around in helicopters.'

Kim laughed. 'That's good. Because I'm never going on a helicopter again – and don't you, either!'

I want to tell Kim that sometimes you don't have a choice in the matter.

The hatch in the helicopter is opened, and my stretcher with all its tubes and lines is loaded in. I climb into the helicopter behind it. A medic bounds in next to me, still pumping the little plastic bulb that is apparently breathing for me. Once we lift off, I understand why Kim got so queasy. A helicopter is not like an airplane, a smooth fast bullet. A helicopter is more like a hockey puck bounced through the sky. Up and down, side to side. I have no idea how these people can work on me, can read the small computer print-outs, can drive this thing while they communicate about me through headsets, how they can do any of it with the chopper chopping around.

The helicopter hits an air pocket and by all rights it should make me queasy. But I don't feel anything, at least the me who's a bystander here does not. And the me on the stretcher doesn't seem to feel anything, either. Again I have to wonder if I'm dead but then I tell myself no. They would not have loaded me on this helicopter, would not be flying me across the lush forests if I were dead.

Also, if I were dead, I like to think Mom and Dad would've come for me by now.

I can see the time on the control panel. It's 10:37. I wonder what's happening back down on the ground. Has Willow figured out who the emergency is? Has anyone phoned my grandparents? They live one town over from us, and I was looking forward to dinner with them. Gramps fishes and he smokes his own salmon and oysters, and we would've probably eaten that with Gran's home-made thick brown beer bread. Then Gran would've taken Teddy over to the giant recycling bins in town and let him swim around for magazines. Lately, he's had a thing for *Reader's Digest*. He likes to cut out the cartoons and make collages.

I wonder about Kim. There's no school today. I probably won't be in school tomorrow. She'll probably think I'm absent because I stayed out late listening to Adam and Shooting Star in Portland.

Portland. I am fairly certain that I'm being taken there. The helicopter pilot keeps talking to Trauma One. Outside the window, I can see the peak of Mount Hood looming. That means Portland is close.

Is Adam already there? He played in Seattle last night but he's always so full of adrenaline after a gig, and driving helps him to come down. The band is normally happy to let him chauffeur while they nap. If he's already in Portland, he's probably still asleep. When he wakes up, will he have coffee on Hawthorne Boulevard? Maybe take a book over to the Japanese Garden? That's what we did the last time I went to Portland with him, only it was warmer then. Later this afternoon, I know that the band will do a sound check. And then Adam will go outside to await my arrival. At first, he'll think that I'm late. How is he going to know that I'm actually early? That I got to Portland this morning while the snow was still melting?

*

'Have you ever heard of this Yo-Yo Ma dude?' Adam asked me. It was the spring of my sophomore year, which was his junior year. By then, Adam had been watching me practice in the music wing for several months. Our school was one of those progressive ones that always got written up in national magazines because of its emphasis on the arts. We did get a lot of free periods to paint in the studio or practice music. I spent mine in the soundproof booths of the music wing. Adam was there a lot, too, playing guitar. Not the electric guitar he played in his band. Just acoustic melodies.

I rolled my eyes. 'Everyone's heard of Yo-Yo Ma.'

Adam grinned. I noticed for the first time that his smile was lopsided, his mouth sloping up on one side. He hooked his ringed thumb out toward the quad. 'I don't think you'll find five people out there who've heard of Yo-Yo Ma. And by the way, what kind of name is that? Is it ghetto or something? Yo Mama?'

'It's Chinese.'

Adam shook his head and laughed. 'I know plenty of Chinese people. They have names like Wei Chin. Or Lee something. Not Yo-Yo Ma.'

'You cannot be blaspheming the master,' I said. But then I laughed in spite of myself. It had taken me a few months to believe that Adam wasn't taking the piss out of me, and after that we'd started having these little conversations in the corridor.

Still, his attention baffled me. It wasn't that Adam was such a popular guy. He wasn't a jock or a most-likely-to-succeed sort. But he was cool. Cool in that he played in a band with people who went to the college in town. Cool in that he had his own rocker-ish style, procured from thrift stores and garage sales, not from Urban Outfitters knock-offs. Cool in that he seemed totally happy to sit in the lunchroom absorbed in a book, not just pretending to read because he didn't have anywhere to sit or anyone to sit with.

That wasn't the case at all. He had a small group of friends and a large group of admirers.

And it wasn't like I was a dork, either. I had friends and a best friend to sit with at lunch. I had other good friends at the music conservatory camp I went to in the summer. People liked me well enough, but they also didn't really know me. I was quiet in class. I didn't raise my hand a lot or sass the teachers. And I was busy, much of my time spent practicing or playing in a string quartet or taking theory classes at the community college. Kids were nice enough to me, but they tended to treat me as if I were a grown-up. Another teacher. And you don't flirt with your teachers.

'What would you say if I said I had tickets to the master?' Adam asked me, a glint in his eyes.

'Shut up. You do not,' I said, shoving him a little harder than I'd meant to.

Adam pretended to fall against the glass wall. Then he dusted himself off. 'I do. At the Schnitzle place in Portland.'

'It's the Arlene Schnitzer Hall. It's part of the Symphony.'

'That's the place. I got tickets. A pair. You interested?'

'Are you serious? Yes! I was dying to go but they're like eighty dollars each. Wait, how did you get tickets?'

'A friend of the family gave them to my parents, but they can't go. It's no big thing,' Adam said quickly. 'Anyhow, it's

Friday night. If you want, I'll pick you up at five-thirty and we'll drive to Portland together.'

'OK,' I said, like it was the most natural thing.

By Friday afternoon, though, I was more jittery than when I'd inadvertently drunk a whole pot of Dad's tar-strong coffee while studying for final exams last winter.

It wasn't Adam making me nervous. I'd grown comfortable enough around him by now. It was the uncertainty. What was this, exactly? A date? A friendly favor? An act of charity? I didn't like being on soft ground any more than I liked fumbling my way through a new movement. That's why I practiced so much, so I could rush myself on solid ground and then work out the details from there.

I changed my clothes about six times. Teddy, a kindergartner back then, sat in my bedroom, pulling the Calvin and Hobbes books down from shelves and pretending to read them. He cracked himself up, though I wasn't sure whether it was Calvin's high jinks or my own making him so goofy.

Mom popped her head in to check on my progress. 'He's just a guy, Mia,' she said when she saw me getting worked up.

'Yeah, but he's just the first guy I've ever gone on a maybe-date with,' I said. 'So I don't know whether to wear date clothes or symphony clothes – do people here even dress up for that kind of thing? Or should I just keep it casual, in case it's *not* a date?'

'Just wear something you feel good in,' she suggested. 'That way you're covered.' I'm sure Mom would've pulled out all the stops had she been me. In the pictures of her and Dad from the early days, she looked like a cross between a 1930s siren and a biker chick, with her pixie haircut, her big blue eyes coated in kohl eyeliner, and her rail-thin body always ensconced in some sexy get-up, like a lacy vintage camisole paired with skintight leather pants.

I sighed. I wished I could be so ballsy. In the end, I chose a long black skirt and a maroon short-sleeved sweater. Plain and simple. My trademark, I guess.

When Adam showed up in a sharkskin suit and Creepers (an ensemble that wholly impressed Dad), I realized that this really was a date. Of course, Adam would choose to dress up for the symphony and a 1960s sharkskin suit could've just been his cool take on formal, but I knew there was more to it than that. He seemed nervous as he shook hands with my dad and told him that he had his band's old CDs. 'To use as coasters, I hope,' Dad said. Adam looked surprised, unused to the parent being more sarcastic than the child, I imagine.

'Don't you kids get too crazy. Bad injuries at the last Yo-Yo Ma mosh pit,' Mom called as we walked down the lawn.

'Your parents are so cool,' Adam said, opening the car door for me.

'I know,' I replied.

We drove to Portland, making small talk. Adam played me snippets of bands he liked, a Swedish pop trio that sounded monotonous but then some Icelandic art band that was quite beautiful. We got a little lost downtown and made it to the concert hall with only a few minutes to spare.

Our seats were in the balcony. Nosebleeds. But you don't go to Yo-Yo Ma for the view, and the sound was incredible. That man has a way of making the cello sound like a crying woman one minute, a laughing child the next. Listening to him, I'm always reminded of why I started playing cello in the first place – that there is something so human and expressive about it.

When the concert started, I peered at Adam out of the corner of my eye. He seemed good-natured enough about the whole thing, but he kept looking at his program, probably counting off the movements until intermission. I worried that he was bored, but after a while I got too caught up in the music to care.

Then, when Yo-Yo Ma played 'Le Grand Tango', Adam reached over and grasped my hand. In any other context, this would have been cheesy, the old yawn-and-cop-a-feel move. But Adam wasn't looking at me. His eyes were closed and he was swaying slightly in his seat. He was lost in the music, too. I squeezed his hand back and we sat there like that for the rest of the concert.

Afterward, we bought coffees and doughnuts and walked along the river. It was misting and he took off his suit jacket and draped it over my shoulders.

'You didn't really get those tickets from a family friend, did you?' I asked.

I thought he would laugh or throw up his arms in mock surrender like he did when I beat him in an argument. But he looked straight at me, so I could see the green and browns and grays swimming around in his irises. He shook his head. 'That was two weeks of pizza-delivery tips,' he admitted.

I stopped walking. I could hear the water lapping below. 'Why?' I asked. 'Why me?'

'I've never seen anyone get as into music as you do. It's why I like to watch you practice. You get the cutest crease in your forehead, right there,' Adam said, touching me above the bridge of my nose. 'I'm obsessed with music and even I don't get transported like you do.'

'So, what? I'm like a social experiment to you?' I meant it to be jokey, but it came out sounding bitter.

'No, you're not an experiment,' Adam said. His voice was husky and choked.

I felt the heat flood my neck and I could sense myself blushing. I stared at my shoes. I knew that Adam was looking at me now with as much certainty as I knew that if I looked up he was going to kiss me. And it took me by surprise how much I wanted to be kissed by him, to realize that I'd thought about it so often that I'd memorized the exact shape of his lips, that I'd imagined running my finger down the cleft of his chin.

My eyes flickered upward. Adam was there waiting for me.

That was how it started.

12:19 p.m.

There are a lot of things wrong with me.

Apparently, I have a collapsed lung. A ruptured spleen. Internal bleeding of unknown origin. And most serious, the contusions on my brain. I've also got broken ribs. Abrasions on my legs, which will require skin grafts; and on my face, which will require cosmetic surgery – but, as the doctors note, that is only if I am lucky.

Right now, in surgery, the doctors have to remove my

spleen, insert a new tube to drain my collapsed lung, and stanch whatever else might be causing the internal bleeding. There isn't a lot they can do for my brain.

'We'll just wait and see,' one of the surgeons says, looking at the CAT scan of my head. 'In the meantime, call down to the blood bank. I need two units of O neg and keep two units ahead.'

O negative. My blood type. I had no idea. It's not like it's something I've ever had to think about before. I've never been in the hospital unless you count the time I went to the emergency room after I cut my ankle on some broken glass. I didn't even need stitches then, just a tetanus shot.

In the operating room, the doctors are debating what music to play, just like we were in the car this morning. One guy wants jazz. Another wants rock. The anesthesiologist, who stands near my head, requests classical. I root for her, and I feel like that must help because someone pops on a Wagner CD, although I don't know that the rousing 'Ride of the Valkyries' is what I had in mind. I'd hoped for something a little lighter. *Four Seasons*, perhaps.

The operating room is small and crowded, full of blindingly bright lights, which highlight how grubby this place is. It's nothing like on TV, where operating rooms are like pristine theaters that could accommodate an opera singer, *and* an audience. The floor, though buffed shiny, is dingy with scuff marks and rust streaks, which I take to be old bloodstains.

Blood. It is everywhere. It does not faze the doctors one bit. They slice and sew and suction through a river of it, like they are washing dishes in soapy water. Meanwhile, they pump an ever-replenishing stock into my veins.

The surgeon who wanted to listen to rock sweats a lot. One of the nurses has to periodically dab the perspiration from his face with gauze that she holds in tongs. At one point, he sweats through his mask and has to replace it.

The anesthesiologist has gentle fingers. She sits at my head, keeping an eye on all my vitals, adjusting the amounts of the fluids and gases and drugs they're giving me. She must be doing a good job because I don't appear to feel anything, even though they are yanking at my body. It's rough and messy work, nothing like that game Operation we used to play as kids where you had to be careful not touch the sides as you removed a bone, or the buzzer would go off.

The anesthesiologist absentmindedly strokes my temples through her latex gloves. This is what Mom used to do when I came down with the flu or got one of those headaches that hurt so bad I used to imagine cutting open a vein in my temple just to relieve the pressure.

The Wagner CD has repeated twice now. The doctors decide it's time for a new genre. Jazz wins. People always assume that because I am into classical music, I'm a jazz aficionado. I'm not. Dad is. He loves it, especially the wild, latter-day Coltrane stuff. He says that jazz is punk for old people. I guess that explains it, because I don't like punk, either.

The operation goes on and on. I'm exhausted by it. I don't know how the doctors have the stamina to keep up. They're standing still, but it seems harder than running a marathon.

I start to zone out. And then I start to wonder about this state I'm in. If I'm not dead – and the heart monitor is bleeping along, so I assume I'm not – but I'm not in my body, either, can I go anywhere? Am I a ghost? Could I transport myself to a beach in Hawaii? Can I pop over to Carnegie Hall in New York City? Can I go to Teddy?

Just for the sake of experiment, I wiggle my nose like Samantha on *Bewitched*. Nothing happens. I snap my fingers. Click my heels. I'm still here.

I decide to try a simpler maneuver. I walk into the wall, imagining that I'll float through it and come out the other side. Except that what happens when I walk into the wall is that I hit a wall.

A nurse bustles in with a bag of blood, and before the door shuts behind her, I slip through it. Now I'm in the hospital corridor. There are lots of doctors and nurses in blue and green scrubs hustling around. A woman on a gurney, her hair in a gauzy blue shower cap, an IV in her arm, calls out to 'William, William.' I walk a little farther. There are rows of operating rooms, all full of sleeping people. If the patients inside these rooms are like me, why then can't I see the people outside the people? Is everyone else loitering about like I seem to be? I'd really like to meet someone in my condition. I have some questions, like, what is this state I'm in exactly and how do I get out of it? How do I get back to my body? Do I have to wait for the doctors to wake me up? But there's no one else like me around. Maybe the rest of them figured out how to get to Hawaii.

I follow a nurse through a set of automatic double doors. I'm in a small waiting room now. My grandparents are here.

Gran is chattering away to Gramps, or maybe just to the air. It's her way of not letting emotion get the best of her. I've seen her do it before, when Gramps had a heart attack. She is wearing her wellies and her gardening smock, which is smudged with mud. She must have been working in her greenhouse when she heard about us. Gran's hair is short and curly and gray; she's been wearing it in a permanent wave, Dad says, since the 1970s. 'It's easy,' Gran says. 'No muss, no fuss.' This is so typical of her. No nonsense. She's so quintessentially practical that most people would never guess she has a thing for angels. She keeps a collection of ceramic angels, yarn-doll angels, blown-glass angels, you-name-it angels, in a special china hutch in her sewing room. And she doesn't just collect angels; she believes in them. She thinks that they're everywhere. Once, a pair of loons nested in the pond in the woods behind their house. Gran was convinced that it was her long-dead parents, come to watch over her.

Another time, we were sitting outside on her porch and I saw a red bird. 'Is that a red crossbill?' I'd asked Gran.

She'd shaken her head. 'My sister Gloria is a crossbill,' Gran had said, referring to my recently deceased great-aunt Glo, with whom Gran had never gotten along. 'She wouldn't be coming around here.'

Gramps is staring into the dregs of his Styrofoam cup, peeling away the top of it so that little white balls collect in his lap. I can tell it's the worst kind of swill, the kind that looks like it was brewed in 1997 and has been sitting on a burner ever since. Even so, I wouldn't mind a cup.

You can draw a straight line from Gramps to Dad to Teddy, although Gramps's wavy hair has gone from blond to gray and he is stockier than Teddy, who is a stick, and Dad, who is wiry and muscular from afternoon weight-lifting sessions at the local YMCA gym. But they all have the same watery gray-blue eyes, the color of the ocean on a cloudy day.

Maybe this is why I now find it hard to look at Gramps.

*

Juilliard was Gran's idea. She's from Massachusetts originally, but she moved to Oregon in 1955, on her own. Now that would be no big deal, but I guess fifty-two years ago it was kind of scandalous for a twenty-two-year-old unmarried woman to do that kind of thing. Gran claimed she was drawn to wild open wilderness and it didn't get more wild than the endless forests and craggy beaches of Oregon. She got a job as a secretary working for the Forest Service. Gramps was working there as a biologist.

We go back to Massachusetts sometimes in the summers, to a lodge in the western part of the state that for one week is taken over by Gran's extended family. That's when I see the second cousins and great aunts and uncles whose names I barely recognize. I have lots of family in Oregon, but they're all from Gramps's side.

Last summer at the Massachusetts retreat, I brought my cello so I could keep up my practicing for an upcoming chamber music concert. The flight wasn't full, so the stewardesses let it travel in a seat next to me, just like the pros do it. Teddy thought this was hilarious and kept trying to feed it pretzels.

At the lodge, I gave a little concert one night, in the main room, with my relatives and the dead game animals mounted on the wall as my audience. It was after that that someone mentioned Juilliard, and Gran became taken with the idea.

At first, it seemed far-fetched. There was a perfectly good music program at the university near us. And, if I wanted to stretch, there was a conservatory in Seattle, which was only a few hours' drive. Juilliard was across the country. And expensive. Mom and Dad were intrigued with the idea of it, but I could tell neither one of them really wanted to relinquish me to New York City or go into hock so that I could maybe become a cellist for some second-rate small-town orchestra. They had no idea whether I was good enough. In fact, neither did I. Professor Christie told me that I was one of the most promising students she'd ever taught, but she'd never mentioned Juilliard to me. Juilliard was for virtuoso musicians, and it seemed arrogant to even think that they'd give me a second glance.

But after the retreat, when someone else, someone impartial and from the East Coast, deemed me Juilliard-worthy, the idea burrowed into Gran's brain. She took it upon herself to speak to Professor Christie about it, and my teacher took hold of the idea like a terrier to a bone.

So, I filled out my application, collected my letters of recommendation, and sent in a recording of my playing. I didn't tell Adam about any of this. I had told myself that it was because there was no point advertising it when even getting an audition was such a long shot. But even then I'd recognized that for the lie that it was. A small part of me felt like even applying was some kind of betrayal. Juilliard was in New York. Adam was here.

But not at high school anymore. He was a year ahead of me, and this past year, my senior year, he'd started at the university in town. He only went to school part-time now because Shooting Star was starting to get popular. There was a record deal with a Seattle-based label, and a lot of traveling to gigs. So only after I got the creamy envelope embossed with THE JUILLIARD SCHOOL and a letter inviting me to audition did I tell Adam that I'd applied and been granted an audition. I explained how many people didn't get that far. At first he looked a little awestruck, like he couldn't quite believe it. Then he gave a sad little smile. 'Yo Mama better watch his back,' he said.

The auditions were held in San Francisco. Dad had some big conference at the school that week and couldn't get away, and Mom had just started a new job at the travel agency, so Gran volunteered to accompany me. 'We'll make a girls' weekend of it. Take high tea at the Fairmont. Go window-shopping in Union Square. Ride the ferry to Alcatraz. We'll be tourists.'

But a week before we were due to leave, Gran tripped over a tree root and sprained her ankle. She had to wear one of those clunky boots and wasn't supposed to walk. Minor panic ensued. I said I could just go by myself – drive, or take the train, and come right back.

It was Gramps who insisted on taking me. We drove down together in his pickup truck. We didn't talk much, which was fine by me because I was so nervous. I kept fingering the Popsicle-stick good-luck talisman Teddy had presented me with before we left. 'Break an arm,' he'd told me.

Gramps and I listened to classical music and farm reports on the radio when we could pick up a station. Otherwise, we sat in silence. But it was such a calming silence; it made me relax and feel closer to him than any heart-to-heart would have.

Gran had booked us in a really frilly inn, and it was funny to see Gramps in his work boots and plaid flannel amid all the lacy doilies and potpourri. But he took it all in stride.

The audition was grueling. I had to play five pieces: a Shostakovich concerto, two Bach suites, all Tchaikovsky's *Pezzo capriccioso*, which was next to impossible, and a movement from Ennio Morricone's *The Mission*, a fun but risky choice because Yo-Yo Ma had covered this and everyone would compare. I walked out with my legs wobbly and my underarms wet with sweat. But my endorphins were surging and that, combined with the huge sense of relief, left me totally giddy.

'Shall we see the town?' Gramps asked, his lips twitching into a smile.

'Definitely!'

We did all the things Gran had promised we would do. Gramps took me to high tea and shopping, although for dinner, we skipped out on the reservations Gran had made at some fancy place on Fisherman's Wharf and instead wandered into Chinatown, looking for the restaurant with the longest line of people waiting outside, and ate there.

When we got back home, Gramps dropped me off and enveloped me in a hug. Normally, he was a handshaker, maybe a back patter on really special occasions. His hug was strong and tight, and I knew it was his way of telling me that he'd had a wonderful time.

'Me, too, Gramps,' I whispered.

3:47 p.m.

They just moved me out of the recovery room into the trauma intensive-care unit, or ICU. It's a horseshoe-shaped room with about a dozen beds and a cadre of nurses, who constantly bustle around, reading the computer print-outs that churn out from the feet of our beds recording our vital signs. In the middle of the room are more computers and a big desk, where another nurse sits.

I have two nurses who check in on me, along with the endless round of doctors. One is a taciturn doughy man with blond hair and a mustache, who I don't much like. And the other is a woman with skin so black it's blue and a lilt in her voice. She calls me 'sweetheart' and perpetually straightens the blankets around me, even though it's not like I'm kicking them off.

There are so many tubes attached to me that I cannot count them all: one down my throat breathing for me; one down my nose, keeping my stomach empty; one in my vein, hydrating me; one in my bladder, peeing for me; several on my chest, recording my heartbeat; another on my finger, recording my pulse. The ventilator that's doing my breathing has a soothing rhythm like a metronome, in, out, in, out.

No one, aside from the doctors and nurses and a social worker, has been in to see me. It's the social worker who speaks to Gran and Gramps in hushed sympathetic tones. She tells them that I am in 'grave' condition. I'm not entirely sure what that means – grave. On TV, patients are always critical, or stable. Grave sounds bad. Grave is where you go when things don't work out here.

'I wish there was something we could do,' Gran says. 'I feel so useless just waiting.'

'I'll see if I can get you in to see her in a little while,' the social worker says. She has frizzy gray hair and a coffee stain on her blouse; her face is kind. 'She's still sedated from the surgery and she's on a ventilator to help her breathe while her body heals from the trauma. But it can be helpful even for patients in a comatose state to hear from their loved ones.'

Gramps grunts in reply.

'Do you have any people you can call?' the social worker asks. 'Relatives who might like to be here with you. I understand this must be quite a trial for you, but the stronger you can be, the more it will help Mia.'

I startle when I hear the social worker say my name. It's a jarring reminder that it's me they're talking about. Gran tells her about the various people who are en route right now, aunts, uncles. I don't hear any mention of Adam.

Adam is the one I really want to see. I wish I knew where he was so I could try to go there. I have no idea how he's going to find out about me. Gran and Gramps don't have his phone number. They don't carry cell phones, so he can't call them. And I don't know how he'd even know to call them. The people who would normally pass along pertinent information that something has happened to me are in no position to do that.

I stand over the bleeping tubed lifeless form that is me. My skin is gray. My eyes are taped shut. I wish someone would take the tape off. It looks like it itches. The nice nurse bustles over. Her scrubs have lollipops on them, even though this isn't a pediatric unit. 'How's it going, sweetheart?' she asks me, as if we just bumped into each other in the grocery store.

*

It didn't start out so smoothly with Adam and me. I think I had this notion that love conquers all. And by the time he dropped me off from the Yo-Yo Ma concert, I think we were both aware that we were falling in love. I thought that getting to this part was the challenge. In books and movies, the stories always end when the two people finally have their romantic kiss. The happily-ever-after part is just assumed.

It didn't quite work that way for us. It turned out that coming from such far corners of the social universe had its downsides. We continued to see each other in the music wing, but these interactions remained platonic, as if neither one of us wanted to mess with a good thing. But whenever we met at other places in the school – when we sat together in the cafeteria or studied side by side on the quad on a sunny day – something was off. We were uncomfortable.

Conversation was stilted. One of us would say something and the other would start to say something else at the same time.

'You go,' I'd say.

'No, you go,' Adam would say.

The politeness was painful. I wanted to push through it, to return to the glow of the night of the concert, but I was unsure of how to get back there.

Adam invited me to see his band play. This was even worse than school. If I felt like a fish out of water in my family, I felt like a fish on Mars in Adam's circle. He was always surrounded by funky, lively people, by cute girls with dyed hair and piercings, by aloof guys who perked up when Adam rock-talked with them. I couldn't do the groupie thing. And I didn't know how to rock talk at all. It was a language I should've understood, being both a musician and Dad's daughter, but I didn't. It was like how Mandarin speakers can sort of understand Cantonese but not really, even though non-Chinese people assume all Chinese can communicate with one another, even though Mandarin and Cantonese are actually different.

I dreaded going to shows with Adam. It wasn't that I was jealous. Or that I wasn't into his kind of music. I loved to watch him play. When he was onstage, it was like the guitar was a fifth limb, a natural extension of his body. And when he came offstage afterward, he would be sweaty but it was such a clean sweat that part of me was tempted to lick the side of his face, like it was a lollipop. I didn't, though.

Once the fans would descend, I'd skitter off to the sidelines. Adam would try to draw me back, to wrap an arm around my waist, but I'd disentangle myself and head back to the shadows.

'Don't you like me anymore?' Adam chided me after one show. He was kidding, but I could hear the hurt behind the offhand question.

'I don't know if I should keep coming to your shows,' I said.

'Why not?' he asked. This time he didn't try to disguise the hurt.

'I feel like I keep you from basking in it all. I don't want you to have to worry about me.'

Adam said that he didn't mind worrying about me, but I could tell that part of him did.

We probably would've broken up in those early weeks were it not for my house. At my house, with my family, we found a common ground. After we'd been together for a month, I took Adam home with me for his first family dinner with us. He sat in the kitchen with Dad, rock-talking. I observed, and

I still didn't understand half of it, but unlike at the shows didn't feel left out.

'Do you play basketball?' Dad asked. When it came to observing sports, Dad was a baseball fanatic, but when it came to playing, he loved to shoot hoops.

'Sure,' Adam said. 'I mean, I'm not very good.'

'You don't need to be good; you just need to be committed. Want to play a quick game? You already have your basketball shoes on,' Dad said, looking at Adam's Converse high-tops. Then he turned to me. 'You mind?'

'Not at all,' I said, smiling. 'I can practice while you play.'

They went out to the courts behind the nearby elementary school. They returned forty-five minutes later. Adam was covered with a sheen of sweat and looking a little dazed.

'What happened?' I asked. 'Did the old man whoop you?'

Adam shook his head and nodded at the same time. 'Well, yes. But it's not that. I got stung by a bee on my palm while we were playing. Your dad grabbed my hand and sucked the venom out.'

I nodded. This was a trick he'd learned from Gran, and unlike with rattlesnakes, it actually worked on bee stings. You got the stinger and the venom out, so you were left with only a little itch.

Adam broke into an embarrassed smile. He leaned in and whispered into my ear: 'I think I'm a little wigged out that

I've been more intimate with your dad than I have with you.'

I laughed at that. But it was sort of true. In the few weeks we'd been together, we hadn't done much more than kiss. It wasn't that I was a prude. I *was* a virgin, but I certainly wasn't devoted to staying that way. And Adam certainly wasn't a virgin. It was more that our kissing had suffered from the same painful politeness as our conversations.

'Maybe we should remedy that,' I murmured.

Adam raised his eyebrows as if asking me a question. I blushed in response. All through dinner, we grinned at each other as we listened to Teddy, who was chattering about the dinosaur bones he'd apparently dug up in the back garden that afternoon. Dad had made his famous salt roast, which was my favorite dish, but I had no appetite. I pushed the food around my plate, hoping no one would notice. All the while, this little buzz was building inside me. I thought of the tuning fork I used to adjust my cello. Hitting it sets off vibrations in the note of A – vibrations that keep growing, and growing, until the harmonic pitch fills up the room. That's what Adam's grin was doing to me during dinner.

After the meal, Adam took a quick peek at Teddy's fossil finds, and then we went upstairs to my room and closed the door. Kim is not allowed to be alone in her house with boys

51

– not that the opportunity ever came up. My parents had never mentioned any rules on this issue, but I had a feeling that they knew what was happening with Adam and me, and even though Dad liked to play it all *Father Knows Best*, in reality, he and Mom were suckers when it came to love.

Adam lay down on my bed, stretching his arms above his head. His whole face was grinning – eyes, nose, mouth. 'Play me,' he said.

'What?'

'I want you to play me like a cello.'

I started to protest that this made no sense, but then I realized it made perfect sense. I went to my closet and grabbed one of my spare bows. 'Take off your shirt,' I said, my voice quavering.

Adam did. As thin as he was, he was surprisingly built. I could've spent twenty minutes staring at the contours and valleys of his chest. But he wanted me closer. I wanted me closer.

I sat down next to him on the bed, perpendicular to his hips, so his long body was stretched out in front of me. The bow trembled as I placed it on the bed. I reached with my left hand and caressed Adam's head as if it were the scroll of my cello. He smiled again and closed his eyes. I relaxed a little. I fiddled with his ears as though they were the string pegs and then I playfully tickled him as he laughed softly. I placed two fingers on his Adam's apple. Then, taking a deep breath for courage, I plunged into his chest. I ran my hands up and down the length of his torso, focusing on the sinews in his muscles, assigning each one a string – A, G, C, D. I traced them down, one at a time, with the tip of my fingers. Adam got quiet then, as if he were concentrating on something.

I reached for the bow and brushed it across his hips, where I imagined the bridge of the cello would be. I played lightly at first and then with more force and speed as the song now playing in my head increased in intensity. Adam lay perfectly still, little groans escaping from his lips. I looked at the bow, looked at my hands, looked at Adam's face, and felt this surge of love, lust, and an unfamiliar feeling of power. I had never known that I could make someone feel this way.

When I finished, he stood up and kissed me long and deep. 'My turn,' he said. He pulled me to my feet and started by slipping the sweater over my head and edging down my jeans. Then he sat down on the bed and laid me across his lap. At first Adam did nothing except hold me. I closed my eyes and tried to feel his eyes on my body, seeing me as no one else ever had.

Then he began to play.

He strummed chords across the top of my chest, which tickled and made me laugh. He gently brushed his hands, moving farther down. I stopped giggling. The tuning fork intensified – its vibrations growing every time Adam touched me somewhere new.

After a while he switched to more of a Spanish-style, finger-picking type of playing. He used the top of my body as the fret board, caressing my hair, my face, my neck. He plucked at my chest and my belly, but I could feel him in places his hands were nowhere near. As he played on, the energy magnified; the tuning fork going crazy now, firing off vibrations all over, until my entire body was humming, until I was left breathless. And when I felt like I could not take it one more minute, the swirl of sensations hit a dizzying crescendo, sending every nerve ending in my body on high alert.

I opened my eyes, savoring the warm calm that was sweeping over me. I started to laugh. Adam did, too. We kissed for a while longer until it was time for him to go home.

As I walked him out to his car, I wanted to tell him that I loved him. But it seemed like such a cliché after what we'd just done. So I waited and told him the next day. 'That's a relief. I thought you might just be using me for sex,' he joked, smiling.

After that, we still had our problems, but being overly polite with each other wasn't one of them.

4:39 p.m.

It's almost a crowd now. Gran and Gramps. Uncle Greg. Aunt Diane. Aunt Kate. My cousins Heather and John and David. Dad is one of five kids, so there are still lots more relatives out there. Nobody is talking about Teddy, which leads me to believe that he's not here. He's probably still at the other hospital, being taken care of by Willow.

The relatives gather in the hospital waiting room. Not the little one on the surgical floor where Gran and Gramps were during my operation, but a larger one on the hospital's main floor that is tastefully decorated in shades of mauve and has comfy chairs and sofas and magazines that are almost current. Everyone still talks in hushed tones, as if being respectful of the other people waiting, even though it's only my family in the waiting room. It's all so serious, so ominous. I go back into the hallway to get a break.

I'm so happy when Kim arrives; happy to see the familiar sight of her long black hair in a single braid. She wears the braid every day and always, by lunch time, the curls and ringlets of her thick mane have managed to escape in rebellious little tendrils. But she refuses to surrender to that hair of hers, and every morning, it goes back into the braid.

Kim's mother is with her. She doesn't let Kim drive long distances, and I guess that after what's happened, there's no way she'd make an exception today. Mrs Schein is red-faced and blotchy, like she's been crying or is about to cry. I know this because I have seen her cry many times. She's very emotional. 'Drama queen,' is how Kim puts it. 'It's the Jewish-mother gene. She can't help it. I suppose I'll be like that one day, too,' Kim concedes.

Kim is so the opposite of that, so droll and funny in a low-key way that she's always having to say 'just kidding' to people who don't get her sarcastic sense of humor, that I cannot imagine her ever being like her mother. Then again, I don't have much basis for comparison. There are not a lot of Jewish mothers in our town or that many Jewish kids at our school. And the kids who are Jewish are usually only half, so all it means is that they have a menorah alongside their Christmas trees.

But Kim is really Jewish. Sometimes I have Friday-night dinner with her family when they light candles, eat braided bread, and drink wine (the only time I can imagine neurotic Mrs Schein allowing Kim to drink). Kim's expected to only date Jewish guys, which means she doesn't date. She jokes that this is the reason her family moved here, when in fact it was because her father was hired to run a computer-chip plant. When she was thirteen, she had a bat mitzvah at a temple in Portland, and during the candle-lighting ceremony at the reception, I got called up to light one. Every summer, she goes to Jewish sleepaway camp in New Jersey. It's called Camp Torah Habonim, but Kim calls it *Torah Whore*, because all the kids do all summer is hook up.

'Just like band camp,' she joked, though my summer conservatory program is nothing like *American Pie*.

Right now I can see Kim is annoyed. She's walking fast, keeping a good ten feet between her and her mother as they march down the halls. Suddenly her shoulders go up like a cat that's just spied a dog. She swerves to face her mother.

'Stop it!' Kim demands. 'If I'm not crying, there's no fucking way you're allowed to.'

Kim never curses. So this shocks me.

'But,' Mrs Schein protests, 'how can you be so . . .' – sob – 'so calm when—'

'Cut it out!' Kim interjects. 'Mia is still here. So I'm not losing it. And if I don't lose it, you don't get to!'

Kim stalks off in the direction of the waiting room, her mother following limply behind. When they reach the waiting room and see my assembled family, Mrs Schein starts sniffling.

Kim doesn't curse this time. But her ears go pink, which

is how I know she's still furious. 'Mother. I am going to leave you here. I'm taking a walk. I'll be back later.'

I follow her back out into the corridor. She wanders around the main lobby, loops around the gift shop, visits the cafeteria. She looks at the hospital directory. I think I know where she's headed before she does.

There's a small chapel in the basement. It's hushed in there, a library kind of quiet. There are plush chairs like the kind you find at a movie theater, and a muted soundtrack playing some New-Agey type music.

Kim slumps back in one of the chairs. She takes off her coat, the one that is black and velvet and that I have coveted since she bought it at some mall in New Jersey on a trip to visit her grandparents.

'I love Oregon,' she says with a hiccup attempt at a laugh. I can tell by her sarcastic tone that it's me she's talking to, not God. 'This is the hospital's idea of nondenominational.' She points around the chapel. There is a crucifix mounted on the wall, a flag of a cross draped over the lectern, and a few paintings of the Madonna and Child hanging in the back. 'We have a token Star of David,' she says, gesturing to the six-pointed star on the wall. 'But what about the Muslims? No prayer rugs or symbol to show which way is east toward Mecca? And what about the Buddhists? Couldn't they spring for a gong? I mean there are probably more Buddhists than Jews in Portland anyway.'

I sit down in a chair beside her. It feels so natural the way that Kim is talking to me like she always does. Other than the paramedic who told me to hang in there and the nurse who keeps asking me how I'm doing, no one has talked to me since the accident. They talk about me.

I've never actually seen Kim pray. I mean, she prayed at her bat mitzvah and she does the blessings at Shabbat dinner, but that is because she has to. Mostly, she makes light of her religion. But after she talks to me for a while, she closes her eyes and moves her lips and murmurs things in a language I don't understand.

She opens her eyes and wipes her hands together as if to say *Enough of that*. Then she reconsiders and adds a final appeal. 'Please don't die. I can understand why you'd want to, but think about this: If you die, there's going to be one of those cheesy Princess Diana memorials at school, where everyone puts flowers and candles and notes next to your locker.' She wipes away a renegade tear with the back of her hand. 'I know you'd hate that kind of thing.'

*

Maybe it was because we were too alike. As soon as Kim showed up on the scene, everyone assumed we'd be best friends just because we were both dark, quiet, studious and, at least outwardly, serious. The thing was, neither one of us was a particularly great student (straight B averages all around) or, for that matter, all that serious. We were serious about certain things – music in my case, art and photography in hers – and in the simplified world of junior high school, that was enough to set us apart as separated twins of some sort.

Immediately we got shoved together for everything. On Kim's third day of school, she was the only person to volunteer to be a team captain during a soccer match in PE, which I'd thought was beyond suck-uppy of her. As she put on her red jersey, the coach scanned the class to pick Team B's captain, his eyes settling on me, even though I was one of the least athletic girls. As I shuffled over to put on my jersey, I brushed past Kim, mumbling 'thanks a lot.'

The following week, our English teacher paired us together for a joint oral discussion on *To Kill a Mockingbird*. We sat across from each other in stony silence for about ten minutes. Finally, I said, 'I guess we should talk about racism in the Old South, or something.'

Kim ever so slightly rolled her eyes, which made me want to throw a dictionary at her. I was caught off guard by how intensely I already hated her. 'I read this book at my old school,' she said. 'The racism thing is kind of obvious. I think the bigger thing is people's goodness. Are they naturally good and turned bad by stuff like racism or are we naturally bad and need to work hard not to be?'

'Whatever,' I said. 'It's a stupid book.' I didn't know why I'd said that because I'd actually loved the book and had talked to Dad about it; he was using it for his student teaching. I hated Kim even more for making me betray a book I loved.

'Fine. We'll do your idea, then,' Kim said, and when we got a B minus, she seemed to gloat about our mediocre grade.

After that, we just didn't talk. That didn't stop teachers from pairing us together or everyone in the school from assuming that we were friends. The more that happened, the more we resented it – and each other. The more the world shoved us together, the more we shoved back – and against each other. We tried to pretend the other didn't exist even though the existence of our nemeses kept us both occupied for hours.

I felt compelled to give myself reasons why I hated Kim: She was a Goody Two-shoes. She was annoying. She was a show-off. Later, I found out that she did the same thing about me, though her major complaint was that she thought I was a bitch. And one day, she even wrote it to me. In English class, someone flung a folded-up square of notebook paper onto the floor next to my right foot. I picked it up and opened it. It read, *Bitch!*

Nobody had ever called me that before, and though I was automatically furious, deep down I was also flattered that I had elicited enough emotion to be worthy of the name. People called Mom that a lot, probably because she had a hard time holding her tongue and could be brutally blunt when she disagreed with you. She'd explode like a thunderstorm, and then be fine again. Anyhow, she didn't care that people called her a bitch. 'It's just another word for feminist,' she told me with pride. Even Dad called her that sometimes, but always in a jokey, complimentary way. Never during a fight. He knew better.

I looked up from my grammar book. There was only one person who would've sent this note to me, but I still scarcely believed it. I peered at the class. Everyone had their faces in their books. Except for Kim. Her ears were so red that it made the little sideburn-like tendrils of dark hair look like they were also blushing. She was glaring at me. I might have been eleven years old and a little socially immature, but I recognized a gauntlet being thrown down when I saw it, and I had no choice but to take it up.

When we got older, we liked to joke that we were so glad we had that fist fight. Not only did it cement our friendship but it also provided us our first and likely *only* opportunity for a good brawl. When else were two girls like us going to come to blows? I wrestled on the ground with Teddy, and sometimes I pinched him, but a fist fight? He was just a baby, and even if he were older, Teddy was like half kid brother and half my own kid. I'd been babysitting him since he was a few weeks old. I could never hurt him like that. And Kim, an only child, didn't have any siblings to sock. Maybe at camp she could've gotten into a scuffle, but the consequences would've been dire: hours-long conflict-resolution seminars with the counselors and the rabbi. 'My people know how to fight with the best of them, but with words, with lots and lots of words,' she told me once.

But that fall day, we fought with fists. After the last bell, without a word, we followed each other out to the play-ground, dropped our backpacks on the ground, which was wet from the day's steady drizzle. She charged me like a bull, knocking the wind out of me. I punched her on the side of the head, fist closed, like men do. A crowd of kids gathered around to witness the spectacle. Fighting was novelty enough at our school. Girl-fighting was extra special. And good girls going at it was like hitting the jackpot.

By the time teachers separated us, half of the sixth grade was watching us (in fact, it was the ring of students loiter-ing that alerted the playground monitors that something was up). The fight was a tie, I suppose. I had a split lip and a bruised wrist, the latter inflicted upon myself when my swing at Kim's shoulder missed her and landed squarely on the pole of the volleyball net. Kim had a swollen eye and a bad scrape on her thigh as a result of her tripping over her backpack as she attempted to kick me.

There was no heartfelt peacemaking, no official détente. Once the teachers separated us, Kim and I looked at each other and started laughing. After finagling ourselves out of a visit to the principal's office, we limped home. Kim told me that the only reason that she volunteered for team captain was that if you did that at the beginning of a school year, coaches tended to remember and that actually kept them from picking you in the future (a handy trick I co-opted from then on). I explained to her that I actually agreed with her take on *To Kill a Mockingbird*, which was one of my favorite books. And then that was it. We were friends, just as everyone had assumed all along that we would be. We never laid a hand on each other again, and even though we'd get into plenty of verbal clashes, our tiffs tended to end the way our fist fight had, with us cracking up.

After our big brawl, though, Mrs Schein refused to let Kim come over to my house, convinced that her daughter would return on crutches. Mom offered to go over and smooth things out, but I think that Dad and I both realized that given her temper, her diplomatic mission might end up with a restraining order against our family. In the end, Dad invited the Scheins over for a roast-chicken dinner, and though you could see Mrs Schein was still a little weirded out by my family – 'So you work in a record store while you study to become a teacher? And *you* do the cooking? How unusual,' she said to Dad – Mr Schein declared my parents decent and our family non-violent and told Kim's mother that Kim ought to be allowed to come and go freely.

For those few months in sixth grade, Kim and I shed our good-girl personas. Talk about our fight circulated, the details growing more exaggerated – broken ribs, torn-off fingernails, bite marks. But when we came back to school after winter break, it was all forgotten. We were back to being the dark, quiet, good-girl twins.

We didn't mind anymore. In fact, over the years that reputation has served us well. If, for instance, we were both absent on the same day, people automatically assumed we had come down with the same bug, not that we'd ditched school to watch art films being shown in the film-survey class at the university. When, as a prank, someone put our school up for sale, covering it with signs and posting a listing on eBay, suspicious eyes turned to Nelson Baker and Jenna McLaughlin, not to us. Even if we had owned up to the prank – as we'd planned to if anyone else got in trouble – we'd have had a hard time convincing anyone it really was us.

This always made Kim laugh. 'People believe what they want to believe,' she said.

4:47 p.m.

Mom once snuck me into a casino. We were going on vacation to Crater Lake and we stopped at a resort on an Indian reservation for the buffet lunch. Mom decided to do a bit of gambling, and I went with her while Dad stayed with Teddy, who was napping in his stroller. Mom sat down at the dollar blackjack tables. The dealer looked at me, then at Mom, who returned his mildly suspicious glance with a look sharp enough to cut diamonds followed by a smile more brilliant than any gem. The dealer sheepishly smiled back and didn't say a word. I watched Mom play, mesmerized. It seemed like we were in there for fifteen minutes but then Dad and Teddy came in search of us, both of them grumpy. It turned out we'd been there for over an hour.

The ICU is like that. You can't tell what time of day it is or how much time has passed. There's no natural light. And there's a constant soundtrack of noise, only instead of the electronic beeping of slot machines and the satisfying jangle of quarters, it's the hum and whir of all the medical equipment, the endless muffled pages over the PA, and the steady talk of the nurses.

I'm not entirely sure how long I've been in here. A while ago, the nurse I liked with the lilting accent said she was going home. 'I'll be back tomorrow, but I want to see you here, sweetheart,' she said. I thought that was weird at first. Wouldn't she want me to be home, or moved to another part of the hospital? But then I realized that she meant she wanted to see me in this ward, as opposed to dead.

The doctors keep coming around and pulling up my eyelids and waving around a flashlight. They are rough and hurried, like they don't consider eyelids worthy of gentleness. It makes you realize how little in life we touch one another's eyes. Maybe your parents will hold an eyelid up to get out a piece of dirt, or maybe your boyfriend will kiss your eyelids, light as a butterfly, just before you drift off to sleep. But eyelids are not like elbows or knees or shoulders, parts of the body accustomed to being jostled.

The social worker is at my bedside now. She is looking through my chart and talking to one of the nurses who normally sits at the big desk in the middle of the room. It is amazing the ways they watch you here. If they're not waving penlights in your eyes or reading the print-outs that come tumbling out from the bedside printers, then they are watching your vitals from a central computer screen. If anything goes slightly amiss, one of the monitors starts bleeping. There is always an alarm going off somewhere. At first, it scared me, but now I realize that half the time, when the alarms go off, it's the machines that are malfunctioning, not the people.

The social worker looks exhausted, as if she wouldn't mind crawling into one of the open beds. I am not her only sick person. She has been shuttling back and forth between patients and families all afternoon. She's the bridge between the doctors and the people, and you can see the strain of balancing between those two worlds.

After she reads my chart and talks to the nurses, she goes back downstairs to my family, who have stopped talking in hushed tones and are now all engaged in solitary activities. Gran is knitting. Gramps is pretending to nap. Aunt Diane playing sudoku. My cousins are taking turns on a GameBoy, the sound turned to mute.

Kim has left. When she came back to the waiting room after visiting the chapel, she found Mrs Schein a total wreck. She'd seemed so embarrassed and had hustled her mother out. Actually, I think having Mrs Schein there probably helped. Comforting her gave everyone else something to do, a way to feel useful. Now they're back to feeling useless, back to the endless wait.

When the social worker walks into the waiting room,

everyone stands up, like they're greeting royalty. She gives a half smile, which I've seen her do several times already today. I think it's her signal that everything is OK, or status quo, and she's just here to deliver an update, not to drop a bomb.

'Mia is still unconscious, but her vital signs are improving,' she tells the assembled relatives, who have abandoned their distractions haphazardly on the chairs. 'She's in with the respiratory therapists right now. They're running tests to see how her lungs are functioning and whether she can be weaned off the ventilator.'

'That's good news, then?' Aunt Diane asks. 'I mean if she can breathe on her own, then she'll wake up soon?'

The social worker gives a practiced sympathetic nod. 'It's a good step if she can breathe on her own. It shows her lungs are healing and her internal injuries are stabilizing. The question mark is still the brain contusions.'

'Why is that?' Cousin Heather interrupts.

'We don't know when she will wake up on her own, or the extent of the damage to her brain. These first twenty-four hours are the most critical and Mia is getting the best possible care.'

'Can we see her?' Gramps asks.

The social worker nods. 'That's why I'm here. I think it would be good for Mia to have a short visit. Just one or two people.'

'We'll go,' Gran says, stepping forward. Gramps is by her side.

'Yes, that's what I thought,' the social worker says. 'We won't be long,' she says to the rest of the family.

The three of them walk down the hall in silence. In the elevator, the social worker attempts to prepare my grandparents for the sight of me, explaining the extent of my external injuries, which look bad, but are treatable. It's the internal injuries that they're worried about, she says.

She's acting like my grandparents are children. But they're tougher than they look. Gramps was a medic in Korea. And Gran, she's always rescuing things: birds with broken wings, a sick beaver, a deer hit by a car. The deer went to a wildlife sanctuary, which is funny because Gran usually hates deer; they eat up her garden. 'Pretty rats,' she calls them. 'Tasty rats' is what Gramps calls them when he grills up venison steaks. But that one deer, Gran couldn't bear to see it suffer, so she rescued it. Part of me suspects she thought it was one of her angels.

Still, when they come through the automatic double doors into the ICU both of them stop, as if repelled by an invisible barrier. Gran takes Gramps's hand, and I try to remember if I've ever seen them hold hands before. Gran scans the beds for me, but just as the social worker starts to point out where I am, Gramps sees me and he strides across the floor to my bed.

'Hello, duck,' he says. He hasn't called me that in ages, not since I was younger than Teddy. Gran walks slowly to where I am, taking little gulps of air as she comes. Maybe those wounded animals weren't such good prep after all.

The social worker pulls over two chairs, setting them up at the foot of my bed. 'Mia, your grandparents are here.' She motions for them to sit down. 'I'll leave you alone now.'

'Can she hear us?' Gran asks. 'If we talk to her, she'll understand?'

'Truly, I don't know,' the social worker responds. 'But your presence can be soothing so long as what you say is sooth-ing.' Then she gives them a stern look, as if to tell them not to say anything bad to upset me. I know it's her job to warn them about things like this and that she is busy with a thousand things and can't always be so sensitive, but for a second, I hate her.

After the social worker leaves, Gran and Gramps sit in silence for a minute. Then Gran starts prattling on about the orchids she's growing in her greenhouse. I notice that she's changed out of her gardening smock into a clean pair of corduroy pants and a sweater. Someone must have stopped by her house to bring her fresh clothes. Gramps is sitting very still, and his hands are shaking. He's not much of a

71

talker, so it must be hard for him being ordered to chat with me now.

Another nurse comes by. She has dark hair and dark eyes brightened with lots of shimmery eye make-up. Her nails are acrylic and have heart decals on them. She must have to work hard to keep her nails so pretty. I admire that.

She's not my nurse but she comes up to Gran and Gramps just the same. 'Don't you doubt for a second that she can hear you,' she tells them. 'She's aware of everything that's going on.' She stands there with her hands on her hips. I can almost picture her snapping gum. Gran and Gramps stare at her, lapping up what she's telling them. 'You might think that the doctors or nurses or all this is running the show,' she says, gesturing to the wall of medical equipment. 'Nuh-uh. *She's* running the show. Maybe she's just biding her time. So you talk to her. You tell her to take all the time she needs, but to come on back. You're waiting for her.'

*

Mom and Dad would never call Teddy or me mistakes. Or accidents. Or surprises. Or any of those other stupid euphemisms. But neither one of us was planned, and they never tried to hide that.

Mom got pregnant with me when she was young. Not teenager-young, but young for their set of friends. She was twenty-three and she and Dad had already been married for a year.

In a funny way, Dad was always a bow-tie wearer, always a little more traditional than you might imagine. Because even though he had blue hair and tattoos and wore leather jackets and worked in a record store, he wanted to marry Mom back at a time when the rest of their friends were still having drunken one-night stands. '*Girlfriend* is such a stupid word,' he said. 'I couldn't stand calling her that. So, we had to get married, so I could call her "wife".'

Mom, for her part, had a messed-up family. She didn't go into the gory details with me, but I knew her father was long gone and for a while she had been out of touch with her mother, though now we saw Grandma and Papa Richard, which is what we called Mom's stepfather, a couple of times a year.

So Mom was taken not just with Dad but with the big, mostly intact, relatively normal family he belonged to. She agreed to marry Dad even though they'd been together just a year. Of course, they still did it their way. They were married by a lesbian justice of the peace while their friends played a guitar-feedback-heavy version of 'The Wedding March.' The bride wore a white fringed flapper dress and black spiked boots. The groom wore leather.

*   *   *

They got pregnant with me because of someone else's wedding. One of Dad's music buddies who'd moved to Seattle had gotten his girlfriend pregnant, so they were doing the shotgun thing. Mom and Dad went to the wedding, and at the reception, they got a little drunk and back at the hotel weren't as careful as usual. Three months later there was a thin blue line on the pregnancy test.

The way they tell it, neither felt particularly ready to be parents. Neither one felt like an adult yet. But there was no question that they would have me. Mom was adamantly pro-choice. She had a bumper sticker on the car that read IF YOU CAN'T TRUST ME WITH A CHOICE, HOW CAN YOU TRUST ME WITH A CHILD? But in her case the choice was to keep me.

Dad was more hesitant. More freaked out. Until the minute the doctor pulled me out and then he started to cry.

'That's poppycock,' he would say when Mom recounted the story. 'I did no such thing.'

'You didn't cry then?' Mom asked in sarcastic amusement.

'I *teared*. I did not cry.' Then Dad winked at me and pantomimed weeping like a baby.

Because I was the only kid in Mom and Dad's group of friends, I was a novelty. I was raised by the music community, with dozens of aunties and uncles who took me in as their own little foundling, even after I started showing a strange preference for classical music. I didn't want for real family, either. Gran and Gramps lived nearby, and they were happy to take me for weekends so Mom and Dad could act wild and stay out all night for one of Dad's shows.

Around the time I was four, I think my parents realized that they were actually doing it – raising a kid – even though they didn't have a ton of money or 'real' jobs. We had a nice house with cheap rent. I had clothes (even if they were hand-me-downs from my cousins) and I was growing up happy and healthy. 'You were like an experiment,' Dad said. 'Surprisingly successful. We thought it must be a fluke. We needed another kid as a kind of control group.'

They tried for four years. Mom got pregnant twice and had two miscarriages. They were sad about it, but they didn't have the money to do all the fertility stuff that people do. By the time I was nine, they'd decided that maybe it was for the best. I was becoming independent. They stopped trying.

As if to convince themselves how great it was not to be tied down by a baby, Mom and Dad bought us tickets to go visit New York for a week. It was supposed to be a musical pilgrimage. We would go to the infamous punk club CBGB's and Carnegie Hall. But when to her surprise, Mom discovered she was pregnant, and then to her greater surprise, stayed pregnant past the first trimester, we had to cancel the trip. She was tired and sick to her stomach and so grumpy

Dad joked that she'd probably scare the New Yorkers. Besides, babies were expensive and we needed to save.

I didn't mind. I was excited about a baby. And I knew that Carnegie Hall wasn't going anywhere. I'd get there someday.

5:40 p.m.

I am a little freaked out right now. Gran and Gramps left a while ago, but I stayed behind here in the ICU. I am sitting in one the chairs, going over their conversation, which was very nice and normal and non-disturbing. Until they left. As Gran and Gramps walked out of the ICU, with me following, Gramps turned to Gran and asked: 'Do you think she decides?'

'Decides what?'

Gramps looked uncomfortable. He shuffled his feet. 'You know? Decides,' he whispered.

'What are you talking about?' Gran sounded exasperated and tender at the same time.

'I don't know what I'm talking about. You're the one who believes in all the angels.'

'What does that have to do with Mia?' Gran asked.

'If they're gone now, but still here, like you believe, what if they want her to join them? What if she wants to join them?'

'It doesn't work like that,' Gran snapped.

'Oh,' was all Gramps said. The inquiry was over.

After they left, I was thinking that one day maybe I'll tell Gran that I never much bought into her theory that birds and such could be people's guardian angels. And now I'm more sure than ever that there's no such thing.

My parents aren't here. They are not holding my hand, or cheering me on. I know them well enough to know that if they could, they would. Maybe not both of them. Maybe Mom would stay with Teddy while Dad watched over me. But neither of them is here.

And it's while contemplating this that I think about what the nurse said. *She's running the show.* And suddenly I understand what Gramps was really asking Gran. He had listened to that nurse, too. He got it before I did.

If I stay. If I live. It's up to me.

All this business about medically induced comas is just doctor talk. It's not up to the doctors. It's not up to the absentee angels. It's not even up to God who, if He exists, is nowhere around right now. It's up to me.

How am I supposed to decide this? How can I possibly stay without Mom and Dad? How can I leave without Teddy? Or Adam? This is too much. I don't even understand how it all works, why I'm here in the state that I'm in or how to get out of it if I wanted to. If I were to say, *I want to wake up*, would I wake up right now? I already tried snapping my heels to find Teddy and trying to beam myself to Hawaii, and that didn't work. This seems a whole lot more complicated.

But in spite of that, I believe it's true. I hear the nurse's words again. I am running the show. Everyone is waiting on me.

I decide. I know this now.

And this terrifies me more than anything else that has happened today.

Where the hell is Adam?

*

A week before Halloween of my junior year, Adam showed up at my door triumphant. He was holding a dress bag and wearing a shit-eating grin.

'Prepare to writhe in jealousy. I just got the best costume,' he said. He unzipped the bag. Inside was a frilly white shirt, a pair of breeches, and a long wool coat with epaulets.

'You're going to be Seinfeld with the puffy shirt?' I asked.

'Pff. *Seinfeld*. And you call yourself a classical musician. I'm going to be Mozart. Wait, you haven't seen the shoes.' He reached into the bag and pulled out clunky black leather numbers with metal bars across the tops.

'Nice,' I said. 'I think my mom has a pair like them.'

'You're just jealous because you don't have such a rockin' costume. And I'll be wearing tights, too. I'm just that secure in my manhood. Also, I have a wig.'

'Where'd you get all this?' I asked, fingering the wig. It felt like it was made of burlap.

'Online. Only a hundred bucks.'

'You spent a hundred dollars on a Halloween costume?'

And the mention of the world *Halloween* Teddy zoomed down the stairs, ignoring me and yanking on Adam's wallet chain. 'Wait here!' he demanded and then ran back upstairs and returned a few seconds later holding a bag. 'Is this a good costume? Or will it make me look babyish?' Teddy asked, pulling out a pitchfork, a set of devil ears, a red tail and a pair of red feetie pajamas.

'Ohh.' Adam stepped backward, his eyes wide. 'That outfit scares the hell out of me and you aren't even wearing it.'

'Really? You don't think the pajamas make it look dumb. I don't want anyone to laugh at me,' Teddy declared, his eye-brows furrowed in seriousness.

I grinned at Adam, who was trying to swallow his own smile. 'Red pajamas plus pitchfork plus devil ears and pointy tail is so fully satanic no one would dare challenge you, lest they risk eternal damnation,' Adam assured him.

Teddy's face broke into a wide grin, showing off the gap of his missing front tooth. 'That's kind of what Mom said, but I just wanted to make sure she wasn't just telling me that so I wouldn't bug her about the costume. You're taking me trick-or-treating, right?' He looked at me now.

'Just like every year,' I answered. 'How else am I gonna get candy?'

'You're coming, too?' he asked Adam.

'I wouldn't miss it.'

Teddy turned on his heel and whizzed back up the stairs. Adam turned to me. 'That's Teddy settled. What are you wearing?'

'Ahh, I'm not much of a costume girl.'

Adam rolled his eyes. 'Well, become one. It's Halloween, our first one together. Shooting Star has a big show that night. It's a costume concert, and you promised to go.'

Inwardly, I groaned. After six months with Adam, I had just gotten used to us being the odd couple at school – people called us Groovy and the Geek. And I was starting to become more comfortable with Adam's bandmates, and had even learned a few words of rock talk. I could hold my own now when Adam took me to the House of Rock, the rambling house near the college where the rest of the band all lived. I could even participate in the band's punk-rock pot-luck parties when everyone invited had to bring something from their fridge that was on the verge of spoiling. We took all the ingredients and made something out of it. I was actually pretty good at finding ways to turn the vegetarian ground beef, beets, feta cheese and apricots into something edible.

But I still hated the shows and hated myself for hating them. The clubs were smoky, which hurt my eyes and made my clothes stink. The speakers were always turned up so high that the music blared, causing my ears ring so loudly afterward that the high-pitched drone would actually keep me up. I'd lie in bed, replaying the awkward night and feeling shittier about it with each playback.

'Don't tell me you're gonna back out,' Adam said, looking equal parts hurt and irritated.

'What about Teddy? We promised we'd take him trick-or-treating—'

'Yeah, at five o'clock. We don't have to be at the show until ten. I doubt even Master Ted could trick-or-treat for five solid hours. So you have no excuse. And you'd better get a good outfit together because I'm going to look hot, in an eighteenth-century kind of way.'

After Adam left to go to work delivering pizzas, I had a pit in my stomach. I went upstairs to practice the Dvořák piece Professor Christie had assigned me, and to work out what was bothering me. Why didn't I like his shows? Was it because Shooting Star was getting popular and I was jealous? Did the ever-growing masses of girl groupies put me off? This seemed like a logical enough explanation, but it wasn't it.

After I'd played for about ten minutes, it came to me: My aversion to Adam's shows had nothing to do with music or groupies or envy. It had to with the doubts. The same niggling doubts I always had about not belonging. I didn't feel like I belonged with my family, and now I didn't feel like I belonged with Adam, except unlike my family, who was stuck with me, Adam had chosen me, and this I didn't understand. Why had he fallen for *me*? It didn't make sense. I knew it was music that brought us together in the first place, put us in the same space so we could even get to know each other. And I knew that Adam liked how into music I was. And that he dug my sense of humor, 'so dark you almost miss it,' he said. And, speaking of dark, I knew he had a thing for dark-haired girls because all of his girl-friends had been brunettes. And I knew that when it was the two of us alone together, we could talk for hours, or sit reading side by side for hours, each one plugged into our own iPod, and still feel completely together. I understood all that in my head, but I still didn't believe it in my heart. When I was with Adam, I felt picked, chosen, special, and that just made me wonder *Why me?* even more.

And maybe this was why even though Adam willingly submitted to Schubert symphonies and attended any recital I gave, bringing me stargazer lilies, my favorite flower, I'd still rather have gone to the dentist than to one of his shows. Which was so churlish of me. I thought of what Mom sometimes said to me when I was feeling insecure: 'Fake it till you make it.' By the time I finished playing the piece three times over, I decided that not only would I go to his show, but for once I'd make as much of an effort to understand his world as he did mine.

'I need your help,' I told Mom that night after dinner as we stood side by side doing dishes.

'I think we've established that I'm not very good at trigonometry. Maybe you can try the online tutor thing,' Mom said.

'Not math help. Something else.'

'I'll do my best. What do you need?'

'Advice. Who's the coolest, toughest, hottest rocker girl you can think of?'

'Debbie Harry,' Mom said.

'Tha—'

'Not finished,' Mom interrupted. 'You can't ask me to pick only one. That's so *Sophie's Choice*. Kathleen Hanna. Patti

Smith. Joan Jett. Courtney Love, in her demented destructionist way. Lucinda Williams, even though she's country she's tough as nails. Kim Gordon from Sonic Youth, pushing fifty and still at it. That woman from Cat Power. Joan Armatrading. Why, is this some kind of social-studies project?'

'Kind of,' I answered, toweling off a chipped plate. 'It's for Halloween.'

Mom clapped her soapy hands together in delight. 'You planning on impersonating one of us?'

'Yeah,' I replied. 'Can you help me?'

Mom left work early so we could trawl through vintage-clothing stores. She decided we should go for a pastiche of rocker looks, rather than trying to copy any one artist. We bought a pair of tight, lizard-skin pants. A blond bobbed wig with severe bangs, à la early-eighties Debbie Harry, which Mom streaked with purple Manic Panic. For accessories, we got a black leather armband for one wrist and about two dozen silver bangles for the other. Mom fished out her own vintage Sonic Youth T-shirt – warning me not to take it off lest someone grab it and sell it on eBay for a couple hundred bucks – and the pair of black, pointy-toed leather spiked boots that she'd worn to her wedding.

*　*　*

On Halloween, she did my make-up, thick streaks of black liquid eyeliner that made my eyes look dangerous. White powder that made my skin pale. Blood-red gashes on my lips. A stick-on nose ring. When I looked in the mirror, I saw Mom's face peering back at me. Maybe it was the blond wig, but this was the first time I ever thought I actually looked like any of my immediate family.

My parents and Teddy waited downstairs for Adam while I stayed in my room. It felt like this was prom or something. Dad held the camera. Mom was practically dancing with excitement. When Adam came through door, showering Teddy with Skittles, Mom and Dad called me down.

I did a slinky walk as best as I could in the heels. I'd expected Adam to go crazy when he saw me, his jeans-and-sweaters girlfriend all glammed out. But he smiled his usual greeting, chuckling a bit. 'Nice costume,' was all he said.

'Quid pro quo. Only fair,' I said, pointing to his Mozart ensemble.

'I think you look scary, but pretty,' Teddy said. 'I'd say sexy, too, but I'm your brother, so that's gross.'

'How do you even know what *sexy* means?' I asked. 'You're six.'

'Everyone knows what *sexy* means,' he said.

85

Everyone but me, I guess. But that night, I kind of learned. When we trick-or-treated with Teddy, my own neighbors who'd known me for years didn't recognize me. Guys who'd never given me a second glance did a double take. And every time that happened, I felt a little bit more like the risky sexy chick I was pretending to be. Fake it till you make it actually worked.

The club where Shooting Star was playing was packed. Everyone was in costume, most of the girls in the kinds of racy get-ups – cleavage-bearing French maids, whip-wielding dominatrixes, slutty *Wizard of Oz* Dorothys with skirts hiked up to show their ruby garters – that normally made me feel like a big oaf. I didn't feel oafish at all that night, even if nobody seemed to recognize that I was wearing a costume.

'You were supposed to dress up,' a skeleton guy chastised me before offering me a beer.

'I fucking LOVE those pants,' a flapper girl screamed into my ear. 'Did you get them in Seattle?'

'Aren't you in the Crack House Quartet?' a guy in a Hillary Clinton mask asked me, referring to some hard-core band that Adam loved and I hated.

When Shooting Star went on, I didn't stay backstage, which is what I normally did. Backstage I can sit on a chair and have an uninterrupted view and not have to talk to anybody. This time, I lingered out by the bar, and then, when the flapper girl grabbed me, I joined her dancing in the mosh pit.

I'd never gone into the mosh pit before. I had little interest in running around in circles while drunk, brawny boys in leather trod on my toes. But tonight, I totally got into it. I understood what it was like to merge your energy with the mob's and to absorb theirs as well. How in the pit, when things got going, you weren't so much walking or dancing as being sucked into a whirlpool.

When Adam finished his set, I was as panting and sweaty as he was. I didn't go backstage to greet him before everyone else got to him. I waited for him to go to the floor of the club, to meet his public like he did at the end of every show. And when he came out, a towel around his neck, sucking on a bottle of water, I flung myself into his arms and kissed him open mouthed and sloppy in front of everyone. I could feel him smiling as he kissed me back.

'Well, well, looks like someone has been infused with spirit of Debbie Harry,' he said, wiping some of the lipstick off his chin.

'I guess so. What about you? Are you feeling very Mozarty?'

'All I know about him is from what I saw in that movie. But I remember he was kind of a horndog, so after that kiss,

I guess I am. You ready to go? I can load up and we can get out of here.'

'No, let's stay for the last set.'

'*Really?*' Adam asked, his eyebrows rising in surprise.

'Yeah. I might even go into the pit with you.'

'Have you been drinking?' he teased.

'Just the Kool-Aid,' I replied.

We danced, stopping every now and again to make out, until the club closed.

On the way home, every so often Adam would turn to look at me and smile while shaking his head.

'So you like me like this?' I asked.

'Hmm,' he responded.

'Is that a yes or a no?'

'Of course I like you.'

'No, like this. Did you like me tonight?'

Adam straightened up. 'I liked that you got into the show and weren't chomping to leave ASAP. And I loved dancing with you. And I loved how comfortable you seemed to be with all us riffraff.'

'But did you like me like this? Like me better?'

'Than what?' he asked. He looked genuinely perplexed.

'Than normal.' I was getting irritated now. I'd felt so

brazen tonight, like the Halloween costume had imbued me with a new personality, one more worthy of Adam, of my family. I tried to explain that to him, and to my dismay, found myself near tears.

Adam seemed to sense that I was upset. He pulled the car off onto a logging road and turned to me. 'Mia, Mia, Mia,' he said, stroking the tendrils of my hair that had escaped from the wig. 'This is the you I like. You definitely dressed sexier and are, you know, blond and that's different. But the you who you are tonight is the same you I was in love with yesterday, the same you I'll be in love with tomorrow. I love that you're fragile and tough, quiet and kick-ass. Hell, you're one of the punkest girls I know, no matter who you listen to or what you wear.'

After that, whenever I started to doubt Adam's feelings, I'd think about my wig, gathering dust in my closet, and it would bring back the memory of that night. And then I wouldn't feel insecure. I'd just feel lucky.

7:13 p.m.

He's here.

I have been hanging out in an empty hospital room in the maternity ward, wanting to be far away from my relatives and even farther away from the ICU and that nurse, or more specifically what that nurse said and what I now understand. I needed to be somewhere where people wouldn't be sad, where the thoughts concerned life, not death. So I came here, the land of screaming babies. Actually, the wail of the newborns is comforting. They have so much fight in them already.

But it's quiet in this room now. So I'm sitting on the windowsill, staring out at the night. A car screeches into the parking garage, shaking me out of my reverie. I peer down in time to catch a glimpse of the taillights of a pink car disappear into the darkness. Sarah, who is the girlfriend of Liz, Shooting Star's drummer, has a pink Dodge Dart. I hold my breath, waiting for Adam to appear out of the tunnel. And then he's here, walking up the ramp, hugging his leather jacket against the winter night. I can see the chain of his wallet glinting in the floodlights. He stops, turns around to talk to someone behind him. I see the soft figure of a woman emerge from the shadows. At first, I think it must be Liz. But then I see the braid.

I wish I could hug her. To thank her for always being one step ahead of what I need.

Of course Kim would go to Adam, to tell him in person as opposed to breaking the news over the phone, and then to bring him here, to me. It was Kim who knew that Adam was playing a show in town. Kim who must have somehow managed to cajole her mother into driving downtown. Kim, who judging by Mrs Schein's absence, must have convinced her mother to go home, to let her stay with Adam and me. I remember how it took Kim two months to get permission to take that helicopter flight with her uncle, so I'm impressed that she managed this amount of emancipation within the space of a few hours. It was Kim who must have braved any number of intimidating bouncers and hipsters to find Adam. And Kim who must have braved telling Adam.

I know this sounds ridiculous, but I'm glad it wasn't me. I don't think I could have borne it. Kim had to bear it.

And now, because of her, he is finally here.

All day long, I've been imagining Adam's arrival, and in my fantasy, I rush to greet him, even though he can't see me and even though, from what I can tell so far, it's nothing like that movie *Ghost*, where you can walk through your loved ones so that *they* feel your presence.

But now that Adam is here, I'm paralyzed. I'm scared to see him. To see his face. I've seen Adam cry twice. Once when we watched *It's a Wonderful Life*. And another time when we were in the train station in Seattle and we saw a mother yelling and swatting her son who had Down's Syndrome. He just got quiet and it was only when we were walking away that I saw the tears rolling down his cheeks.

And it damn near tore my heart out. If he is crying, it *will* kill me. Forget this *my choice* business. That alone will do me in.

I'm such a chicken-shit.

I look at the clock on the wall. It's past seven now. Shooting Star will not be opening for Bikini after all. Which is a shame. It was a huge break for them. For a second, I wonder if the rest of the band will go on without Adam. I very much doubt it, though. It's not just that he is the lead singer and the lead guitar player. The band has this kind of code. Loyalty to feelings is important. Last summer, when Liz and Sarah broke up (for what turned out to be all of a month) and Liz was too distraught to play, they canceled their five-night tour, even though this guy Gordon who plays drums in another band offered to sub for her.

I watch Adam make his way to the hospital's main entrance, Kim trailing behind him. Just before he comes to the covered awning and the automatic doors, he looks up into the sky. He is waiting for Kim but I also like to think he's looking for me. His face, illuminated by the lights, is blank, like someone vacuumed away all his personality, leaving only a mask. He doesn't look like him. But at least he's not crying.

That gives me the guts to go to him now. Or rather to me, to the ICU, which is where I know he will want to go. Adam

92

knows Gran and Gramps and the cousins, and I imagine he'll join the waiting-room vigil later. But right now he's here for me.

Back in the ICU time stands still as always. One of the surgeons who worked on me earlier – the one who sweated a lot and, when it was his turn to pick the music, blasted Weezer – is checking in on me.

The light is dim and artificial and kept to the same level all the time, but even so, the circadian rhythms win out and a nighttime hush has fallen over the place. It is less frenetic than it was during the day, like the nurses and machines are all a little tired and have reverted to power-save mode.

So when Adam's voice reverberates from the hallway outside the ICU, it really wakes everyone up.

'What do you mean I can't go in?' he booms.

I make my way across the ICU, standing just on the other side of the automatic doors. I hear the orderly outside explain to Adam that he is not allowed in this part of the hospital.

'This is bullshit!' Adam yells.

Inside the ward, all the nurses look toward the door, their heavy eyes wary. I am pretty sure they're thinking: *Don't we have enough to deal with inside without having to calm down crazy people outside?* I want explain to them that Adam isn't crazy. That he never yells, except for very special occasions.

The graying middle-aged nurse who doesn't attend to the patients but sits by and monitors the computers and phones, gives a little nod and stands up as if accepting a nomination. She straightens her creased white pants and makes her way toward the door. She's really not the best one to talk to him. I wish I could warn them that they ought to send Nurse Ramirez, the one who reassured my grand-parents (and freaked me out). She'd be able to calm him down. But this one is only going to make it worse. I follow her through the double doors where Adam and Kim are arguing with an orderly. The orderly looks at the nurse. 'I told them they're not authorized to be up here,' he explains. The nurse dismisses him with the wave of a hand.

'Can I help you, young man?' she asks Adam. Her voice sounds irritated and impatient, like some of Dad's tenured colleagues at school who Dad says are just counting the days till retirement.

Adam clears his throat, attempting to pull himself together. 'I'd like to visit a patient,' he says, gesturing toward the doors blocking him from the ICU.

'I'm afraid that's not possible,' she replies.

'But my girlfriend, Mia, she's—'

'She's being well cared for,' the nurse interrupts. She

sounds tired, too tired for sympathy, too tired to be moved by young love.

'I understand that. And I'm grateful for it,' Adam says. He's trying his best to play by her rules, to sound mature, but I hear the catch in his voice when he says: 'I really need to see her.'

'I'm sorry, young man, but visits are restricted to immediate family.'

I hear Adam gasp. *Immediate family*. The nurse doesn't mean to be cruel. She's just clueless, but Adam won't know that. I feel the need to protect him and to protect the nurse from what he might do to her. I reach for him, on instinct, even though I cannot really touch him. But his back is to me now. His shoulders are hunched over, his legs starting to buckle.

Kim, who was hovering near the wall, is suddenly at his side, her arms encircling his falling form. With both arms locked around his waist, she turns to the nurse, her eyes blazing with fury. 'You don't understand!' she cries.

'Do I need to call security?' the nurse asks.

Adam waves his hand, surrendering to the nurse, to Kim. '*Don't*,' he whispers to Kim.

So Kim doesn't. Without saying another word, she hoists his arm around her shoulder and shifts his weight onto her. Adam has about a foot and fifty pounds on Kim, but after stumbling for a second, she adjusts to the added burden. She bears it.

*

Kim and I have this theory that almost everything in the world can be divided into two groups.

There are people who like classical music. People who like pop. There are city people. And country people. Coke drinkers. Pepsi drinkers. There are conformists and free-thinkers. Virgins and non-virgins. And there are the kind of girls who have boyfriends in high school, and the kind of girls who don't.

Kim and I had always assumed that we both belonged to the latter category. 'Not that we'll be forty-year-old virgins or anything,' she reassured. 'We'll just be the kinds of girls who have boyfriends in college.'

That always made sense to me, seemed preferable even. Mom was the sort of girl who had had boyfriends in high school and often remarked that she wished she hadn't wasted her time. 'There's only so many times a girl wants to get drunk on cheap beer, go cow-tipping, and make out in the back of a pickup truck. As far as the boys I dated were concerned, that amounted to a romantic evening.'

Dad on the other hand, didn't really date till college. He was shy in high school, but then he started playing drums and freshman year of college joined a punk band, and boom, girlfriends. Or at least a few of them until he met Mom, and boom, a wife. I kind of figured it would go that way for me.

So, it was a surprise to both Kim and me when I wound up in Group A, with the boyfriended girls. At first, I tried to hide it. After I came home from the Yo-Yo Ma concert, I told Kim the vaguest of details. I didn't mention the kissing. I rationalized the omission: There was no point getting all worked up about a kiss. One kiss does not a relationship make. I'd kissed boys before, and usually by the next day the kiss had evaporated like a dewdrop in the sun.

Except I knew that with Adam it *was* a big deal. I knew from the way the warmth flooded my whole body that night after he dropped me off at home, kissing me once more at my doorstep. By the way I stayed up until dawn hugging my pillow. By the way that I could not eat the next day, could not wipe the smile off my face. I recognized that the kiss was a door I had walked through. And I knew that I'd left Kim on the other side.

After a week, and a few more stolen kisses, I knew I had to tell Kim. We went for coffee after school. It was May but it was pouring rain as though it were November. I felt slightly suffocated by what I had to do.

'I'll buy. You want one of your froufrou drinks?' I asked. That was another one of the categories we'd determined:

people who drank plain coffee and people who drank gussied-up caffeine drinks like the mint-chip lattes Kim was so fond of.

'I think I'll try the cinnamon-spice chai latte,' she said, giving me a stern look that said, *I will not be ashamed of my beverage selection.*

I bought us our drinks and a piece of marionberry pie with two forks. I sat down across from Kim, running the fork along the scalloped edge of the flaky crust.

'I have something to tell you,' I said.

'Something about having a boyfriend?' Kim's voice was amused, but even though I was looking down, I could tell that she'd rolled her eyes.

'How'd you know?' I asked, meeting her gaze.

She rolled her eyes again. 'Please. Everyone knows. It's the hottest gossip this side of Melanie Farrow dropping out to have a baby. It's like a Democratic presidential candidate marrying a Republican presidential candidate.'

'Who said anything about marrying?'

'I'm just being metaphoric,' Kim said. 'Anyhow, I know. I knew even before you knew.'

'Bullshit.'

'Come on. A guy like Adam going to a Yo-Yo Ma concert. He was buttering you up.'

'It's not like that,' I said, though of course, it was totally like that.

'I just don't see why you couldn't tell me sooner,' she said in a quiet voice.

I was about to give her my whole one-kiss-not-equaling-a-relationship spiel and to explain that I didn't want to blow it out of proportion, but I stopped myself. 'I was afraid you'd be mad at me,' I admitted.

'I'm not,' Kim said. 'But I will be if you ever lie to me again.'

'OK,' I said.

'Or if you turn into one of those girlfriends, always pony-ing around after her boyfriend, and speaking in the first-person plural. "*We* love the winter. *We* think Velvet Underground is seminal."'

'You know I wouldn't rock-talk to you. First person singular or plural. I promise.'

'Good,' Kim replied. 'Because if you turn into one of those girls, I'll shoot you.'

'If I turn into one of those girls, I'll hand you the gun.'

Kim laughed for real at that, and the tension was broken. She popped a hunk of pie into her mouth. 'How did your parents take it?'

'Dad went through the five phases of grieving – denial, anger, acceptance, whatever – in like one day. I think he's more freaked out that he is old enough to have a daughter who has a boyfriend.' I paused, took a sip of my coffee, letting the word *boyfriend* rest out in the air. 'And he claims he can't believe that I'm dating a musician.'

'You're a musician,' Kim reminded me.

'You know, a punk, pop musician.'

'Shooting Star is emo-core,' Kim corrected. Unlike me, she cared about the myriad pop musical distinctions: punk, indie, alternative, hard-core, emo-core.

'It's mostly hot air, you know, part of his whole bow-tie-Dad thing. I think Dad likes Adam. He met him when he picked me up for the concert. Now he wants me to bring him over for dinner, but it's only been a week. I'm not quite ready for a meet-the-folks moment yet.'

'I don't think I'll ever be ready for that.' Kim shuddered at the thought of it. 'What about your mom?'

'She offered to take me to Planned Parenthood to get the Pill and told me to make Adam get tested for various diseases. In the meantime, she ordered me to buy condoms now. She even gave me ten bucks to start my supply.'

'Have you?' Kim gasped.

'No, it's only been a week,' I said. 'We're still in the same group on that one.'

'For now,' Kim said.

* * *

One other category that Kim and I devised was people who tried to be cool and people who did not. On this one, I thought that Adam, Kim, and I were in the same column, because even though Adam was cool, he didn't try. It was effortless for him. So, I expected the three of us to become the best of friends. I expected Adam to love everyone I loved as much as I did.

And it did work out like that with my family. He practically became the third kid. But it never clicked with Kim. Adam treated her the way that I'd always imagined he would treat a girl like me. He was nice enough – polite, friendly, but distant. He didn't attempt to enter her world or gain her confidence. I suspected he thought she wasn't cool enough and it made me mad. After we'd been together about three months, we had a huge fight about it.

'I'm not dating Kim. I'm dating you,' he said, after I accused him of not being nice enough to her.

'So what? You have lots of female friends. Why not add her to the stable?'

Adam shrugged. 'I don't know. It's just not there.'

'You're such a snob!' I said, suddenly furious.

Adam eyed me with furrowed brows, like I was a math problem on the blackboard that he was trying to figure out. 'How does that make me a snob? You can't force friendship. We just don't have a lot in common.'

'*That's* what makes you a snob! You only like people like you,' I cried. I stormed out, expecting him to follow after me, begging forgiveness, and when he didn't, my fury doubled. I rode my bike over to Kim's house to vent. She listened to my diatribe, her expression purposefully blasé.

'That's just ridiculous that he only likes people like him,' she scolded when I'd finished spewing. 'He likes you, and you're not like him.'

'That's the problem,' I mumbled.

'Well, then deal with that. Don't drag me into your drama,' she said. 'Besides, I don't really click with him, either.'

'You don't?'

'No, Mia. Not everyone swoons for Adam.'

'I didn't mean it like that. It's just that I want you guys to be friends.'

'Yeah, well, I want to live in New York City and have normal parents. As the man said, "You can't always get what you want."'

'But you're two of the most important people in my life.'

Kim looked at my red and teary face and her expression softened into a gentle smile. 'We know that, Mia. But we're from different parts of your life, just like music and me are from different parts of your life. And that's fine. You don't have to choose one or the other, at least not as far as I'm concerned.'

'But I want those parts of my life to come together.'

Kim shook her head. 'It doesn't work that way. Look, I accept Adam because you love him. And I assume he accepts me because you love me. If it makes you feel any better, your love binds us. And that's enough. Me and him don't have to love each other.'

'But I want you to,' I wailed.

'Mia,' Kim said, an edge of warning in her voice signaling the end of her patience. 'You're starting to act like one of those girls. Do you need to get me a gun?'

Later that night, I stopped by Adam's house to say I was sorry. He accepted my apology with a bemused kiss on the nose. And then nothing changed. He and Kim remained cordial but distant, no matter how much I tried to sell them on each another. The funny thing was, I never really bought into Kim's notion that they were somehow bound together through me – until just now when I saw her half carrying him down the hospital corridor.

8:12 p.m.

I watch Kim and Adam disappear down the hall. I mean to follow them but I'm glued to the linoleum, unable to move my phantom legs. It's only after they disappear around a corner that I rouse myself and trail after them, but they've already gone inside the elevator.

By now I've figured out that I don't have any supernatural abilities. I can't float through walls or dive down stairwells. I can only do the things I'd be able do in real life, except that apparently what I do in my world is invisible to everyone else. At least that seems to be the case because no one looks twice when I open doors or hit the elevator button. I can touch things, even manipulate door handles and the like, but I can't really *feel* anything or anybody. It's like I'm experiencing everything through a fishbowl. It doesn't really make sense to me, but then again, nothing that's happening today makes much sense.

I assume that Kim and Adam are headed to the waiting room to join the vigil, but when I get there, my family is not there. There's a stack of coats and sweaters on the chairs and I recognize my cousin Heather's bright-orange down jacket. She lives in the country and likes to hike in the woods, so she says that the neon colors are necessary to keep drunk hunters from mistaking her for a bear.

I look at the clock on the wall. It could be dinner time. I wander back down the halls to the cafeteria, which has the same fried-food, boiled-vegetable stench as cafeterias every-where. Unappetizing smell aside, it's full of people. The tables are crammed with doctors and nurses and nervous-looking medical students in short white jackets and stethoscopes so shiny that they look like toys. They are all chowing down on cardboard pizza and freeze-dried mashed potatoes. It takes me a while to locate my family, huddled around a table. Gran is chatting to Heather. Gramps is paying careful attention to his turkey sandwich.

Aunt Kate and Aunt Diane are in the corner, whispering about something. 'Some cuts and bruises. He was already released from the hospital,' Aunt Kate is saying, and for a second I think she's talking about Teddy and am so excited I could cry. But then I hear her say something about there being no alcohol in his system, how our car just swerved into his lane and some guy named Mr Dunlap says he didn't have time to stop, and then I realize it's not Teddy they're talking about; it's the other driver.

'The police said it was probably the snow, or a deer that caused them to swerve,' Aunt Kate continues. 'And apparently, this lopsided outcome is fairly common. One party is just fine and the other suffers catastrophic injuries . . .' She trails off.

I don't know that I'd call Mr Dunlap 'just fine', no matter how superficial his injuries. I think about what it must be like to be him, to wake up one Tuesday morning and get into your truck to head off to work at the mill or maybe to the feed-supply store or maybe to Loretta's Diner to have eggs over easy. Mr Dunlap, who was maybe perfectly happy or perfectly miserable, married with kids or a bachelor. But whatever and whoever he was early this morning, he isn't that person any longer. His life has changed irrevocably, too. If what my aunt says is true, and the crash wasn't his fault, then he was what Kim would call 'a poor schmuck,' in the wrong place at the wrong time. And because of his bad luck and because he was in his truck, driving eastbound on Route 27 this morning, two kids are now parentless and at least one of them is in grave condition.

How do you live with that? For a second, I have a fantasy of getting better and getting out of here and going to Mr Dunlap's house, to relieve him of his burden, to reassure him that it's not his fault. Maybe we'd become friends.

Of course, it probably wouldn't work like that. It would be awkward and sad. Besides, I still have no idea what I will decide, still have no clue how I would determine to stay or not stay in the first place. Until I figure that out, I have to leave things up to the fates, or to the doctors, or whoever decides these matters when the decider is too confused to choose between the elevator and the stairs.

I *need* Adam. I take a final look for him and Kim but they're not here, so I head back upstairs to the ICU.

* * *

I find them hiding out on the trauma floor, several halls away from the ICU. They're trying to look casual as they test out the doors to various supply closets. When they finally find an unlocked one, they sneak inside. They fumble around in the dark for a light switch. I hate to break it to them, but it's actually back out in the hall.

'I'm not sure this kind of thing works outside of the movies,' Kim tells Adam as she feels along the wall.

'Every fiction has its base in fact,' he tells her.

'You don't really look like the doctor type,' she says.

'I was hoping for orderly. Or maybe janitor.'

'Why would a janitor be in the ICU?' Kim asks. She's a stickler for these kinds of details.

'Broken lightbulb. I don't know. It's all in how you pull it off.'

'I still don't understand why you don't just go to her family?' asks Kim, pragmatic as ever. 'I'm sure her grandparents could explain, could get you in to see Mia.'

Adam shakes his head. 'You know, when the nurse threatened to call security, my first thought was *I'll just call Mia's parents to fix this.*' Adam stops, takes a few breaths. 'It just keeps walloping me over and over, and it's like it's the first time every time,' he says in a husky voice.

'I know,' Kim replies in a whisper.

'Anyhow,' Adam says, resuming his search for the light

switch, 'I can't go to her grandparents. I can't add anything more to their burden. This is something I have to do for myself.'

I'm sure my grandparents would actually be happy to help Adam. They've met him a bunch of times, and they like him a lot. On Christmas, Gran is always sure to make maple fudge for him because he once mentioned how much he liked it.

But I also know that sometimes Adam needs to do things the dramatic way. He is fond of the Grand Gesture. Like saving up two weeks of pizza-delivery tips to take me to Yo-Yo Ma instead of just asking me out on a regular date. Like decorating my windowsill with flowers every day for a week when I was contagious with the chicken pox.

Now I can see that Adam is concentrating on the new task at hand. I'm not sure what exactly he has in mind, but whatever the plan, I'm grateful for it, if only because it's pulled him out of his emotional stupor I saw in the hallway outside the ICU. I've seen him get like this before, when he's writing a new song or is trying to convince me to do something I won't want to do – like go camping with him – and nothing, not a meteorite crashing into the planet, not even a girlfriend in the ICU, can dissuade him.

Besides, it's the girlfriend in the ICU that's necessitating Adam's ruse to begin with. And from what I can guess, it's the oldest hospital trick in the book, taken straight from that movie *The Fugitive*, which Mom and I recently watched on TNT. I have my doubts about it. So does Kim.

'Don't think that nurse might recognize you?' Kim asks. 'You did yell at her.'

'She won't have to recognize me if she doesn't see me. Now I get why you and Mia are such peas in a pod. A pair of Cassandras.'

Adam has never met Mrs Schein, so he doesn't get that implying that Kim is a worrywart is fighting words. Kim scowls, but then I can see her give in. 'Maybe this retarded plan of yours would work better if we could actually see what we're doing.' She fumbles around in her bag and pulls out the cell phone her mother made her start carrying when she was ten – child-GPS, Kim called it – and turned it on. A square of light softens the darkness.

'Now, that's more like the brilliant girl Mia brags about,' Adam says. He turns on his own cell phone and now the room is illuminated by a dull glow.

Unfortunately, the glow shows that the tiny broom closet is full of brooms, a bucket, and a pair of mops, but is lacking any of the disguises that Adam was hoping for. If I could, I would inform them that the hospital has locker rooms, where the doctors and nurses can stow their street clothes and where they change into their scrubs or their lab coats.

The only generic hospital garb sitting around are those embarrassing gowns that they put the patients in. Adam probably could throw on a gown and cruise the hallways in a wheelchair with no one the wiser, but such an outfit would still not get him into the ICU.

'Shit,' Adam says.

'We can keep trying,' Kim says, suddenly the cheerleader. 'There are like ten floors in this place. I'm sure there are other unlocked closets.'

Adam sinks to the floor. 'Nah. You're right. This is stupid. We need to come up with a better plan.'

'You could fake a drug overdose or something so you wind up in the ICU,' Kim says.

'This is Portland. You're lucky if a drug overdose gets you into the ER,' Adam replies. 'No, I was thinking more like a distraction. You know, like making the fire alarm go off so the nurses all come running out.'

'Do you really think sprinklers and panicked nurses are good for Mia?' Kim asks.

'Well, not that exactly, but something so that they all look away for half a second and I stealthily sneak in.'

'They'll find you out right away. They'll throw you out on your backside.'

'I don't care,' Adam responds. 'I only need a second.'

'Why? I mean what can you do in a second?'

Adam pauses for a second. His eyes, which are normally a kind of mutt's mixture of gray and brown and green, have gone dark. 'So I can show her that I'm here. That someone's still here.'

Kim doesn't ask any more questions after that. They sit there in silence, each lost in their own thoughts, and it reminds me of how Adam and I can be together but quiet and separate and I realize that they're friends now, friends for real. No matter what happens, at least I have achieved that.

After about five minutes, Adam knocks on his forehead. 'Of course,' he says.

'What?'

'Time to activate the Bat Signal.'

'Huh?'

'Come on. I'll show you.'

*

When I first started playing the cello, Dad was still playing drums in his band, though that all started to taper off a couple years later when Teddy arrived. But right from the get-go, I could see that there was something different about playing my kind of music, something more than my parents' obvious bewilderment with my classical tastes. My music was solitary. I mean Dad might hammer on his drums for a few hours by himself or write songs alone at the kitchen table, plinking out the notes on his beat-up acoustic guitar, but he always said that songs really got written as you played them. That was what made it so interesting.

When I played, it was most often by myself, in my room. Even when I practiced with the rotating college students, other than during lessons, I still usually played solo. And when I gave a concert or recital, it was alone, on a stage, my cello, myself, and an audience. And unlike Dad's shows, where enthusiastic fans jumped the stage and then dive-bombed into the crowd, there was always a wall between the audience and me. After a while playing like this got lonely. It also got kind of boring.

So in the spring of eighth grade I decided to quit. I planned to trail off quietly, by cutting back my obsessive practices, not giving recitals. I figured that if I laid off gradually, by the time I entered high school in the fall, I could start fresh, no longer be known as 'the cellist.' Maybe then I'd pick up a new instrument, guitar or bass, or even drums. Plus, with Mom too busy with Teddy to notice the length of my cello practice, and Dad swamped with lesson plans and grading papers at his new teaching job, I figured nobody would even realize that I'd stopped playing until it was already a done deal. At least that's what I told myself.

The truth was, I could no sooner quit cello cold turkey than I could stop breathing.

I might have quit for real, were it not for Kim. One afternoon, I invited her to go downtown with me after school.

'It's a weekday. Don't you have practice?' she asked as she twisted the combination on her locker.

'I can skip it today,' I said, pretending to search for my earth-science book.

'Have the pod people stolen Mia? First no recitals. And now you're skipping out on practice. What's going on?'

'I don't know,' I said, tapping my fingers against the locker. 'I'm thinking of trying a new instrument. Like drums. Dad's kit is down in the basement gathering dust.'

'Yeah, right. You on drums. That's rich,' Kim said with a chuckle.

'I'm serious.'

Kim had looked at me, her mouth agape, like I'd just told her I planned on sautéing up a platter of slugs for dinner. 'You can't quit cello,' she said after a moment of stunned silence.

'Why not?'

She looked pained as she tried to explain. 'I don't know but it just seems like your cello is part of who you are. I can't imagine you without that thing between your legs.'

'It's stupid. I can't even play in the school marching band.

I mean, who plays the cello anyhow? A bunch of old people. It's a dumb instrument for a girl to play. It's so dorky. And I want to have more free time, to do fun stuff.'

'What kind of 'fun stuff'?' Kim challenged.

'Um, you know? Shopping. Hanging out with you . . .'

'Please,' Kim said. 'You hate to shop. And you hang out with me plenty. But fine, skip practice today. I want to show you something.' She took me home with her and dragged out a CD of *Nirvana MTV Unplugged* and played me 'Something in the Way'.

'Listen to that,' she said. 'Two guitar players, a drummer, and a *cello player*. Her name is Lori Goldston and I bet when she was younger, she practiced two hours a day like some other girl I know because if you want to play with the philharmonic, or with Nirvana, that's what you have to do. And I don't think anyone would dare call *her* a dork.'

I took the CD home and listened to it over and over for the next week, pondering what Kim said. I pulled my cello out a few times, played along. It was a different kind of music than I'd played before, challenging, and strangely invigorating. I planned to play 'Something in the Way' for Kim the following week when she came over for dinner.

But before I had a chance, at the dinner table Kim casually announced to my parents that she thinks I ought to go to summer camp.

'What, you trying to convert me so I'll go to your Torah camp?' I asked.

'Nope. It's music camp.' She pulled out a glossy brochure for the Franklin Valley Conservatory, a summer program in British Columbia. 'It's for *serious* musicians,' Kim said. 'You have to send a recording of your playing to get in. I called. The deadline for applications is May first, so there's still time.' She turned to face me head-on, as if she were daring me to get mad at her for interfering.

I wasn't mad. My heart was pounding, as if Kim had announced that my family won a lottery and she was about to reveal how much. I looked at her, the nervous look in her eyes betraying the 'you wanna piece of me?' smirk on her face, and I was overwhelmed with gratitude to be friends with someone who often seemed to understand me better than I understood myself. Dad asked me if I wanted to go, and when I protested about the money, he said never mind about that. Did I want to go? And I did. More than anything.

Three months later, when Dad dropped me off in a lonely corner of Vancouver Island, I wasn't so sure. The place looked like a typical summer camp, log cabins in the woods, kayaks strewn on the beach. There were about fifty kids who, judging by the way they were hugging and squealing, had all known one another for years. Meanwhile, I didn't know anybody. For the first six hours, no one talked to me except for the camp's assistant director, who assigned me to a cabin, showed me my bunk bed, and pointed the way to the cafeteria, where that night, I was given a plate of something that appeared to be meat loaf.

I stared miserably at my plate, looking out at the gloomy gray evening. I already missed my parents, Kim, and especially Teddy. He was at that fun stage, wanting to try new things and constantly asking 'What's that?' and saying the most hilarious things. The day before I left, he informed me that he was 'nine-tenths thirsty' and I almost peed myself laughing. Homesick, I sighed and moved the mass of meatloaf around my plate.

'Don't worry, it doesn't rain every day. Just every other day.'

I looked up. There was an impish kid who couldn't have been more than ten years old. He had a blond buzz cut and a constellation of freckles falling down his nose.

'I know,' I said. 'I'm from the Northwest, though it was sunny where I lived this morning. It's the meatloaf I'm worried about.'

He laughed. 'That doesn't get better. But the peanut-butter-and-jelly is always good,' he said, gesturing to a table where a half-dozen kids were fixing themselves sandwiches.

'Peter. Trombone. Ontario,' he said. This, I would learn, was standard Franklin greeting.

'Oh, hey. I'm Mia. Cello. Oregon, I guess.'

Peter told me that he was thirteen, and this was his second summer here; almost everyone started when they were twelve, which is why they all knew one another. Of the fifty students, about half did jazz, the other half classical, so it was a small crew. There were only two other cello players, one of them a tall lanky red-haired guy named Simon who Peter waved over.

'Will you be trying for the concerto competition?' Simon asked me as soon as Peter introduced me as Mia. Cello. Oregon. Simon was Simon. Cello. Leicester, which turned out to be a city in England. It was quite the international group.

'I don't think so. I don't even know what that is,' I answered.

'Well, you know how we all perform in an orchestra for the final symphony?' Peter asked me.

I nodded my head, though really I had only a vague idea. Dad had spent the spring reading out loud from the camp's literature, but the only thing I'd cared about was that I was going to camp with other classical musicians. I hadn't paid too much attention to the details.

'It's the summer's end symphony. People from all over

come to it. It's quite a big deal. We, the youngster musicians, play as a sort of cute sideshow,' Simon explained. 'However, one musician from the camp is chosen to play with the professional orchestra and to perform a solo movement. I came close last year but it went to a flutist. This is my second-to-last chance before I graduate. It hasn't gone to strings in a while, and Tracy, the third of our little trio here, isn't trying out. She's more of a hobby player. Good but not terribly serious. I heard you were serious.'

Was I? Not so serious that I hadn't been on the verge of quitting. 'How'd you hear that?' I asked.

'The teachers hear all the application reels and word gets around. Your audition tape was apparently quite good. It's unusual to admit someone in year two. So I was hoping for some bloody good competition, to up my game, as it were.'

'Whoa, give the girl a chance,' Peter said. 'She's only just tasted the meat loaf.'

Simon shriveled his nose. 'Beg pardon. But if you want to put heads together about audition choices, let's have a little chat about that,' he said, and disappeared off in the direction of the sundae bar.

'Forgive Simon. We haven't had high-quality cellists for a couple of years, so he's excited about new blood. In a purely aesthetic way. He's gay, though it may be hard to tell.'

'Oh. I see. But what did he say? I mean it sounds like he *wants* me to compete against him.'

'Of course he does. That's the fun. That's why we're all at camp in the middle of a flipping rainforest,' he said, gesturing outside. 'That and the amazing cuisine.' Peter looked at me. 'Isn't that why you're here?'

I shrugged. 'I don't know. I haven't played with that many people, at least that many serious people.'

Peter scratched his ears. 'Really? You said you're from Oregon. Ever done anything with the Portland Cello Project?'

'The what?'

'Avant-garde cello collective, eh. Very interesting work.'

'I don't live in Portland,' I mumbled, embarrassed that I'd never even *heard* of any Cello Project.

'Well then, who do you play with?'

'Other people. College students mostly.'

'No orchestra? No chamber-music ensemble? String quartet?'

I shook my head, remembering a time when one of my student teachers invited me to play in a quartet. I'd turned her down because playing one-on-one with her was one thing; playing with complete strangers was another. I'd always believed that the cello was a solitary instrument, but now I was starting to wonder if maybe *I* was the solitary one.

'Hmm. How are you any good?' Peter asked. 'I don't mean to sound like an asshole, but isn't that how you get good? It's like tennis. If you play someone crappy, you end up missing shots or serving all sloppy, but if you play with an ace player, suddenly you're all at the net, lobbing good volleys.'

'I wouldn't know,' I told Peter, feeling like the most boring, sheltered person ever. 'I don't play tennis, either.'

The next few days went by in a blur. I had no idea why they put out the kayaks. There was no time for playing. Not that kind, anyway. The days were totally grueling. Up at six-thirty, breakfast by seven, private study time for three hours in the morning and in the afternoon, and orchestra rehearsal before dinner.

I'd never played with more than a handful of musicians before, so the first few days in orchestra were chaotic. The camp's musical director, who was also the conductor, scrambled to get us situated and then it was everything he could do to get us playing the most basic of movements in any semblance of time. On the third day, he trotted out some Brahms lullabies. The first time we played, it was painful. The instruments didn't blend so much as collide, like rocks caught in a lawn mower. 'Terrible!' he screamed. 'How can any of you ever expect to play in a professional orchestra if you cannot keep time on a lullaby? Now again!'

After about a week, it started to gel and I got my first taste of being a cog in the machine. It made me hear the cello in an entirely new way, how its low tones worked in concert with the viola's higher notes, how it provided a foundation for the woodwinds on the other side of the orchestra pit. And even though you might think that being part of a group would make you relax a little, not care so much how you sounded blended among everyone else, if anything, the opposite was true.

I sat behind a seventeen-year-old viola player named Elizabeth. She was one of the most accomplished musicians in the camp – she'd been accepted into the Royal Conservatory of Music in Toronto – and she was also model-gorgeous: tall, regal, with skin the color of coffee, and cheekbones that could carve ice. I would've been tempted to hate her were it not for her playing. If you're not careful, the viola can make the most awful screech, even in the hands of practiced musicians. But with Elizabeth the sound rang out clean and pure and light. Hearing her play, and watching how deeply she lost herself in the music, I wanted to play like that. Better even. It wasn't just that I wanted to beat her, but also that I felt like I owed it to her, to the group, to myself, to play at her level.

* * *

'That's sounding quite beautiful,' Simon said toward the end of camp as he listened to me practice a movement from Hayden's Cello Concerto No. 2, a piece that had given me no end of trouble when I'd first attempted it last spring. 'Are you using that for the concerto competition?'

I nodded. Then I couldn't help myself, I grinned. After dinner and before lights-out every night, Simon and I had been bringing our cellos outside to hold impromptu concerts in the long twilight. We took turns challenging each other to cello duels, each trying to out-crazy-play the other. We were *always* competing, always trying to see who could play something better, faster, from memory. It had been so much fun, and was probably one reason why I was feeling so good about the Hayden.

'Ahh, someone's awfully confident. Think you can beat me?' Simon asked.

'At soccer. Definitely,' I joked. Simon often told us that he was the black sheep in his family not because he was gay, or a musician, but because he was such a 'shitey footballer'.

Simon pretended that I'd shot him in the heart. Then he laughed. 'Amazing things happen when you stop hiding behind that hulking beast?' he said, gesturing to my cello. I nodded. Simon smiled at me. 'Well, don't go getting quite so cocky. You should hear my Mozart. It sounds like the bloody angels singing.'

Neither one of us won the solo spot that year. Elizabeth did. And though it would take me four more years, eventually I'd nab the solo.

9:06 p.m.

'I've got exactly twenty minutes before our manager has a total shit fit.' Brooke Vega's raspy voice booms in the hospital's now-quiet lobby. So this is Adam's idea: Brooke Vega, the indie-music goddess and lead singer of Bikini. In a trademark punky glam outfit – tonight it's a short bubble skirt, fishnets, high black leather boots, an artfully ripped-up 'Shooting Star' T-shirt, topped off with a vintage fur shrug and a pair of black Jackie O glasses – she stands out in the hospital lobby like an ostrich in a chicken coop. She's surrounded by people: Liz and Sarah; Mike and Fitzy, Shooting Star's rhythm guitarist and bass player, respectively, plus a handful of Portland hipsters who I vaguely recognize. With her magenta hair, she's like the sun, around which her admiring planets revolve. Adam is like a moon, standing off to the side, stroking his chin. Meanwhile, Kim looks shell-shocked, like a bunch of Martians just entered the building. Or maybe it's because Kim worships Brooke Vega. In fact, so does Adam. Aside from me, this was one of the few things they had in common.

'I'll have you out of here in fifteen,' Adam promises, stepping into her galaxy.

She strides toward him. 'Adam, baby,' she croons. 'How you holding up?' Brooke encircles him in a hug as if they are old friends, though I know that they only met for the first time today; just yesterday Adam was saying how nervous he was about it. But now she's here acting like his best friend. That's the power of the scene, I guess. As she embraces Adam, I see every guy and girl in that lobby watching enviously, wishing that they were the ones getting the consolatory cuddle from Brooke.

I can't help but wonder if I were here, if I were watching this as regular old Mia, would I feel jealous, too? Then again, if I were regular old Mia, Brooke Vega would not be in this hospital lobby as part of some great ruse to get Adam in to see me.

'OK, kids. Time to rock-and-roll. Adam, what's the plan?' Brooke asks.

'*You* are the plan. I hadn't really thought beyond you going up to the ICU and making a ruckus.'

Brooke licks her bee-stung lips. 'Making a ruckus is one of my favorite things to do. What do you think we should do? Let out a primal scream? Strip?

Smash a guitar? Wait, I didn't bring my guitar. Damn.'

'You could sing something?' someone suggests.

'How about that old Smiths song 'Girlfriend in a Coma'?' someone calls.

Adam blanches at this sudden reality check and Brooke raises her eyebrows in a stern rebuke. Everyone goes serious.

Kim clears her throat. 'Um, it doesn't do us any good if Brooke is a diversion in the lobby. We need to go upstairs to the ICU and then maybe someone could shout that Brooke Vega is here. That might do it. If it doesn't, then sing. All we really want is to lure a couple of curious nurses out, and that grouchy head nurse after them. Once she comes out of the ICU and sees all of us in the hall, she'll be too busy dealing with us to notice that Adam has slipped inside.'

Brooke appraises Kim. Kim in her rumpled black pants and unflattering sweater. Then Brooke smiles and links arms with my best friend. 'Sounds like a plan. Let's motor, kids.'

I lag behind, watching this procession of hipsters barrel through the lobby. The sheer noisiness of them, of their heavy boots, and loud voices, buzzed on by their sense of urgency, ricochets through the quiet hush of the hospital and breathes some life into the place. I remember watching a TV program once about old-age homes that brought in cats and dogs to cheer the elderly and dying patients. Maybe all hospitals should import groups of rabble-rousing punk rockers to kick-start the languishing patients' hearts.

They stop in front of the elevator, waiting endlessly for one empty enough to ferry them up as a group. I decide that I want to be next to my body when Adam makes it to the ICU. I wonder if I will be able to *feel* his touch on me. While they wait at the elevator banks, I scramble up the stairs.

I've been gone from the ICU for more than two hours, and a lot has changed. There is a new patient in one of the empty beds, a middle-aged man whose face looks like one of those surrealist paintings: half of it looks normal, handsome even, the other half is a mess of blood, gauze, and stitching, like someone just blew it off. Maybe a gunshot wound. We get a lot of hunting accidents around here. One of the other patients, one who was so swaddled in gauze and bandages that I couldn't see if he/she was a man or woman, is gone. In his/her place is a woman whose neck is immobilized in one of those collar things.

As for me, I'm off my ventilator now. I remember the social worker telling my grandparents and Aunt Diane that this was a positive step. I stop to check if I feel any different, but I don't feel anything, not physically anyhow. I haven't since I was in the car this morning, listening to Beethoven's Cello Sonata No. 3. Now that I'm breathing on my own, my wall of machines bleeps far less, so I get fewer visits from the nurses. Nurse Ramirez, the one with the nails, looks over at me every now and again, but she's busy with the new guy with the half face.

'Holy crud. Is that Brooke Vega?' I hear someone ask in a totally fakey dramatic voice from outside the ICU's automatic doors. I've never heard any of Adam's friends talk so PG-13 before. It's their sanitized hospital version of 'holy fucking shit'.

'You mean Brooke Vega of Bikini? Brooke Vega who was on the cover of *Spin* magazine last month? Here in this very hospital?' This time it's Kim talking. She sounds like a six-year-old reciting lines from a school play about the food groups: *You mean you're supposed to eat five servings of fruit and vegetables a day?*

'Yeah, that's right,' says Brooke's raspy voice. 'I'm here to offer some rock-and-roll succor to all the people of Portland.'

A couple of the younger nurses, the ones who probably listen to pop radio or watch MTV and have heard of Bikini, look up, their faces excited question marks. I hear them whispering, eager to see if it's really Brooke, or maybe just happy for the break in the routine.

'Yeah. That's right. So I thought I might sing a little song. One of my favorites. It's called "Eraser",' Brooke says. 'One of you guys want to count me in?'

'I need something to tap with,' Liz answers. 'Anyone got some pens or something?'

Now the nurses and orderlies in the ICU are very curious and heading toward the doors. I'm watching it all play out, like a movie on the screen. I stand next to my bed, my eyes trained on the double doors, waiting for them to open. I'm itching with suspense. I think of Adam, of how calming it feels when he touches me, how when he absent-mindedly strokes the nape of my neck or blows warm air on my cold hands, I could melt into a puddle.

'What's going on?' the older nurse demands. Suddenly every nurse on the floor is looking at her, not out toward Brooke anymore. No one is going to try to explain to her that a famous pop star is outside. The moment has broken. I feel the tension ease into disappointment. The door isn't going to open.

Outside, I hear Brooke start belting out the lyrics to 'Eraser'. Even *a cappella*, even through the automatic double doors, she sounds good.

'Somebody call security now,' the nurse growls.

'Adam, you better just go for it,' Liz yells. 'Now or never. Full-court press.'

'Go!' screams Kim, suddenly an army general. 'We'll cover you.'

The door opens. In tumble more than a half-dozen

punkers, Adam, Liz, Fitzy, some people I don't know, and then Kim. Outside, Brooke is still singing, as though this were the concert she'd come to Portland to give.

As Adam and Kim charge through the door, they both look determined, happy even. I'm amazed by their resilience, by their hidden pockets of strength. I want to jump up and down and root for them like I used to do at Teddy's T-ball games when he'd be rounding third and heading for home. It's hard to believe, but watching Kim and Adam in action, I almost feel happy, too.

'Where is she?' Adam yells. 'Where's Mia?'

'In the corner, next to the supply closet!' someone shouts. It takes me a minute to realize it's Nurse Ramirez.

'Security! Get him! Get him!' the grumpy nurse shouts. She has spotted Adam through all the other invaders and her face has gone pink with anger. Two hospital security guards and two orderlies run inside. 'Dude, was that Brooke Vega?' one asks as he snags Fitzy and flings him toward the exit.

'Think so,' the other answers, grabbing Sarah and steering her out.

Kim has spotted me. 'Adam, she's here!' she screams, and then turns to look at me, the scream dying her throat. '*She's here*,' she says again, only this time it's a whimper.

Adam hears her and he is dodging nurses and making his

way to me. And then he's there at the foot of my bed, his hand reaching out to touch me. His hand about to be on me. Suddenly I think of our first kiss after the Yo-Yo Ma concert, how I didn't know how badly I'd wanted his lips on mine until the kiss was imminent. I didn't realize just how much I was craving his touch, until now that I can almost feel it on me.

Almost. But suddenly he's moving away from me. Two guards have him by the shoulders and have yanked him back. One of the same guards grabs Kim's elbow and leads her out. She's limp now, offering no resistance.

Brooke's still singing in the hallway. When she sees Adam, she stops. 'Sorry, honey,' she says. 'I gotta jet before I miss my show. Or get arrested.' And then she's off down the hall, trailed by a couple of orderlies begging for her autograph.

'Call the police,' the old nurse yells. 'Have him arrested.'

'We're taking him down to security. That's protocol,' one guard says.

'Not up to us to arrest,' the other adds.

'Just get him off my ward.' She harrumphs and turns around. 'Miss Ramirez, that had better not have been you abetting these hoodlums.'

'Of course not. I was in the supply closet. I missed all the hubbub,' she replies. She's such a good liar that her face gives nothing away.

The old nurse claps her hands. 'OK. Show's over. Back to work.'

I bolt back out the ICU door, chasing after Adam and Kim, who are being led into the elevators. I jump in with them. Kim looks dazed, like someone flipped her reset button and she's still booting up. Adam's lips are set in a grim line. I can't tell if he's about to cry or about to punch the guard. For his sake, I hope it's the former. For my own, I hope the latter.

Downstairs, the guards hustle Adam and Kim toward a hallway filled with darkened offices. They're about to go inside one of the few offices with lights on when I hear someone scream Adam's name.

'Adam! Stop. Is that you?'

'Willow?' Adam yells.

'Willow?' Kim mumbles.

'Excuse me, where are you taking them?' Willow yells at the guards as she runs toward them.

'I'm sorry but these two were caught trying to break into the ICU,' one guard explains.

'Only because they wouldn't let us in,' Kim explains weakly.

Willow catches up to them. She's still wearing her nursing clothes, which is strange, because she normally changes out of what she calls 'orthopedic couture' as soon as she can.

Her long, curly auburn hair looks lank and greasy, like she's forgotten to wash it these past few weeks. And her cheeks, normally rosy like apples, have been repainted beige. 'Excuse me. I'm an RN over at Cedar Creek. I did my training here, so if you like we can go straighten this out with Richard Caruthers.'

'Who's he?' one guard asks.

'Director of community affairs,' the other replies. Then he turns to Willow. 'He's not here. It's not business hours.'

'Well, I have his home number,' Willow says, brandishing her cell phone like a weapon. 'I doubt he'd be pleased if I were to call him now and tell him how his hospital was treating someone trying to visit his critically wounded girlfriend. You know that the director values compassion as much as efficiency, and this is not the way to treat a concerned loved one.'

'We're just doing our job, ma'am. Following orders.'

'How about I save you two the trouble and take it from here. The patient's family is all assembled upstairs. They're waiting for these two to join them. Here, if you have any problems, you tell Mr Caruthers to get in touch with me.' She reaches into her bag and pulls out a card and hands it over. One of the guards looks at it, hands it to the other, who stares at it and shrugs.

'Might as well save ourselves the paperwork,' he says. He

lets go of Adam, whose body slumps like a scarecrow taken off his pole. 'Sorry, kid,' he says to Adam, brushing off his shoulders.

'I hope your girlfriend's OK,' the other mumbles. And then they disappear toward the glow of some vending machines.

Kim, who has met Willow all of twice, flings herself into her arms. 'Thank you!' she murmurs into her neck.

Willow hugs her back, pats her on the shoulders before letting go. She rubs her eyes and winces out a brittle laugh. 'What in the hell were you two thinking?' she asks.

'I want to see Mia,' Adam says.

Willow turns to look at Adam and it's like someone has unscrewed her valve, letting all her air escape. She deflates. She reaches out and touches Adam's cheek. 'Of course you do.' She wipes her eyes with the heel of her hand.

'Are you OK?' Kim asks.

Willow ignores the question. 'Let's see about getting you in to Mia.'

Adam perks up when he hears this. 'You think you can? That old nurse has it in for me.'

'If that old nurse is who I think she is, it doesn't matter if she has it in for you. It's not up to her. Let's check in with Mia's grandparents and then I'll find out who's in charge of breaking the rules around here and get you in to see your girl. She needs you now. More than ever.'

Adam swivels around and hugs Willow with such force that her feet lift up off the ground.

Willow to the rescue. Just the way she rescued Henry, Dad's best friend and bandmate, who, once upon a time, was a total drunk playboy. When he and Willow had been dating a few weeks, she told him to straighten out and dry out or say goodbye. Dad said that lots of girls had given Henry ultimatums, tried to force him to settle down, and lots of girls had been left crying on the sidewalk. But when Willow packed her toothbrush and told Henry to grow up, Henry was the one who cried. Then he dried his tears, grew up, got sober and monogamous. Eight years later, here they are, with a baby, no less. Willow is formidable that way. Probably why after she and Henry got together she became Mom's best friend; she was another tough-as-nails, tender-as-kittens, feminist bitch. And probably why she was one of Dad's favorite people, even though she hated the Ramones and thought baseball was boring, while Dad lived for the Ramones and thought baseball was a religious institution.

Now Willow is here. Willow the nurse. Willow who doesn't take no for an answer is here. She'll get Adam in to see me. She'll take care of everything. *Hooray!* I want to shout. *Willow is here!*

I'm so busy celebrating Willow's arrival that the implication of her being here takes a few moments to sink in, but when it does, it hits me like a jolt of electricity.

Willow is here. And if she's here, if she's in my hospital, it means that there isn't any reason for her to be in her hospital. I know her well enough to know that she never would have left him there. Even with me here, she would've stayed with him. He was broken, and brought to her for fixing. He was her patient. Her priority.

I think about the fact that Gran and Gramps are in Portland with me. And that all anyone in that waiting room is talking about is me, how they are avoiding mentioning Mom or Dad or Teddy. I think about Willow's face, which looks like it has been scrubbed clean of all joy. And I think about what she told Adam, that I need him now. More than ever.

And that's how I know. Teddy. He's gone, too.

*

Mom went into labor three days before Christmas, and she insisted we go holiday shopping together.

'Shouldn't you like lie down or go to the birthing center or something?' I asked.

Mom grimaced through a cramp. 'Nah. The contractions aren't that bad and are still like twenty minutes apart. I cleaned our entire house, from top to bottom, while I was in early labor with you.'

'Putting the labor in labor,' I joked.

'You're a smart-ass, you know that?' Mom said. She took a few breaths. 'I've got a ways to go. Now come on. Let's take the bus to the mall. I'm not up to driving.'

'Shouldn't we call Dad?' I asked.

Mom laughed at that. 'Please, it's enough for me to have to birth *this* baby. I don't need to deal with him, too. We'll call him when I'm ready to pop. I'd much rather have you around.'

So Mom and I wandered around the mall, stopping every couple minutes so she could sit down and take deep breaths and squeeze my wrist so hard it left angry red marks. Still, it was a weirdly fun and productive morning. We bought presents for Gran and Gramps (a sweater with an angel on it and a new book about Abraham Lincoln) and toys for the baby and a new pair of rain boots for me. Usually we waited for the holiday sales to buy stuff like that, but Mom said that this year we'd be too busy changing diapers. 'Now's not the time to be cheap. Ow, fuck. Sorry, Mia. Come on. Let's go get pie.'

We went to Marie Callender's for pie. Mom had a slice of pumpkin and of banana cream. I had blueberry. When she was done, she pushed her plate away and announced she was ready to go to the midwife.

We'd never really talked about my being there or not being there. I went everywhere with Mom and Dad at that point, so it was just kind of assumed. We met a nerve-racked Dad at the birthing center, which was nothing like a doctor's office. It was the ground floor of a house, the inside decked out with beds and Jacuzzi tubs, the medical equipment discreetly tucked away. The hippie midwife led Mom inside and Dad asked me if I wanted to come, too. By now, I could hear Mom screaming profanities.

'I can call Gran and she'll pick you up,' Dad said, wincing at Mom's barrage. 'This might take a while.'

I shook my head. Mom needed me. She'd said so. I sat down on one of the floral couches and picked up a magazine with a goofy-looking bald baby on the cover. Dad disappeared into the room with the bed.

'Music! Goddammit! Music!' Mom screamed.

'We have some lovely Enya. Very soothing,' the midwife said.

'Fuck Enya!' Mom screamed. 'Melvins. Earth. Now!'

'I've got it covered,' Dad said. Then he popped a CD of the loudest, churningest, guitar-heaviest music I'd ever heard. It made all the fast-paced punk songs Dad normally listened to sound like harp music. This music was primal and that seemed to make Mom feel better. She started making these low guttural noises. I just sat there quietly. Every so often she'd scream my name and I'd scamper inside. Mom would look up at me, her face plastered with sweat. *Don't be scared*, she'd whisper. *Women can handle the worst kind of pain. You'll find out one day.* Then she'd scream *fuck* again.

I'd seen a couple of births on that cable-TV show, and people usually yelled for a while; sometimes they swore and it had to be bleeped, but it never took longer than half an hour. After three hours, Mom and the Melvins were still screaming along. The whole birthing center felt tropically humid, even though it was forty degrees outside.

Henry dropped by. When he came inside and heard the noise, he froze in his tracks. I knew that the whole kid-thing freaked him out. I'd overheard Mom and Dad talking about that, and Henry's refusal to grow up. He'd apparently been shocked when Mom and Dad had me, and now was completely bewildered that they chose to have a second. They'd both been relieved when he and Willow had gotten back together. 'Finally, a grown-up in Henry's life,' Mom had said.

Henry looked at me; his face was pale and sweaty. 'Holy shit, Mee. Should you be hearing this? Should I be hearing this?'

I shrugged. Henry sat down next to me. 'I've got the flu or something, but your dad just called asking me to bring some food. So here I am,' he said, proffering a Taco Bell bag reeking of onions. Mom let out another moan. 'I should go.

Don't want me spreading germs or anything.' Mom screamed even louder and Henry practically jumped in his seat. 'You sure you wanna hang around for this? You can come back to my place. Willow's there, taking care of me.' He grinned when he mentioned her name. 'She can take care of you, too.' He stood up to leave.

'No. I'm fine. Mom needs me. Dad's kind of freaking out, though.'

'Did he puke yet?' Henry asked, sitting back down on the couch. I laughed, but then saw from his face that he was serious.

'He threw up when you were coming. Almost fainted on the floor. Not that I can blame him. But the dude was a mess, the doctors wanted to kick him out . . . said they were going to if you didn't come out within a half hour. That got your mom so pissed off she pushed you out five minutes later.' Henry smiled, leaning back into the sofa. 'So the story goes. But I'll tell you this: He cried like a mother-fucking baby when you were born.'

'I've heard that part.'

'Heard what part?' Dad asked breathlessly. He grabbed the bag from Henry. 'Taco Bell, Henry?'

'Dinner of champions,' Henry said.

'It'll do. I'm starving. It's intense in there. Got to keep up my strength.'

Henry winked at me. Dad pulled out a burrito and offered one to me. I shook my head. Dad had started unwrapping his meal when Mom let out a growl and then started screaming at the midwife that she was ready to push.

The midwife poked her head out the door. 'I think we're getting close, so maybe you should save dinner for later,' she said. 'Come on back.'

Henry practically bolted out the front door. I followed Dad into the bedroom where Mom was sitting now, panting like a sick dog. 'Would you like to watch?' the midwife asked Dad, but he just swayed and turned a pale shade of green.

'I'm probably better up here,' he said, grasping Mom's hand, which she violently shook off.

No one asked me if I wanted to watch. I just automatically went to stand next to the midwife. It was pretty gross, I'll admit. Lots of blood. And I'd certainly never seen my mom so full-on frontal before. But it felt strangely normal for me to be there. The midwife was telling Mom to push, then hold, then push. 'Go baby, go baby, go baby go,' she chanted. 'You're almost there!' she cheered. Mom looked like she wanted to smack her.

When Teddy slid out, he was head up, facing the ceiling, so that the first thing he saw was me. He didn't come out squalling like you see on TV. He was just quiet. His eyes were open, staring straight at me. He held my gaze as the midwife suctioned out his nose. 'It's a boy,' she shouted.

The midwife put Teddy on Mom's belly. 'Do you want to cut the cord?' she asked Dad. Dad waved his hands no, too overcome or nauseous to speak.

'I'll do it,' I offered.

The midwife held the cord taut and told me where to cut. Teddy lay still, his gray eyes wide open, still staring at me.

Mom always said that it was because Teddy saw me first, and because I cut his cord, that somewhere deep down he thought I was his mother. 'It's like those goslings,' Mom joked. 'Imprinting on a zoologist, not the mama goose, because he was the first one they saw when they hatched.'

She exaggerated. Teddy didn't really think I was his mother, but there were certain things that only I could do for him. When he was a baby and going through his nightly fussy period, he'd only calm down after I played him a lullaby on my cello. When he started getting into *Harry Potter*, only I was allowed to read a chapter to him every night. And when he'd skin a knee or bump his head, if I was around he would not stop crying until I bestowed a magic kiss on the injury, after which he'd miraculously recover.

I know that all the magic kisses in the world probably

couldn't have helped him today. But I would do anything to have been able to give him one.

10:40 p.m.

I run away.

I leave Adam, Kim, and Willow in the lobby and I just start careening through the hospital. I don't realize I'm looking for the pediatric ward until I get there. I tear through the halls, past rooms with nervous four-year-olds sleeping restlessly before tomorrow's tonsillectomies, past the neonatal ICU with babies the size of fists, hooked up to more tubes than I am, past the pediatric oncology unit where bald cancer patients sleep under cheerful murals of rainbows and balloons. I'm looking for him, even though I know I won't find him. Still, I have to keep looking.

I picture his head, his tight blond curls. I love to nuzzle my face in those curls, have done since he was a baby. I keep waiting for the day when he'll swat me away, say 'You're embarrassing me,' the way he does to Dad when Dad cheers too loudly at T-ball games. But so far, that hadn't happened. So far, I've been allowed constant access to that head of his. So far. Now there is no more so far. It's over.

I picture myself nuzzling his head one last time, and I

can't even imagine it without seeing myself crying, my tears turning his blond curlicues straight.

Teddy is never going to graduate from T-ball to baseball. He's never going to grow a mustache. Never going to get into a fist fight or shoot a deer or kiss a girl or have sex or fall in love or get married or father his own curly-haired child. I'm only ten years older than him, but it's like I've already had so much more life. It is unfair. If one of us should have been left behind, if one of us should be given the opportunity for more life, it should be him.

I race through the hospital like a trapped wild animal. *Teddy?* I call. *Where are you? Come back to me!*

But he won't. I know it's fruitless. I give up and drag myself back to my ICU. I want to break the double doors. I want to smash the nurses' station. I want it all to go away. I want to go away. I don't want to be here. I don't want to be in this hospital. I don't want to be in this suspended state where I can see what's happening, where I'm aware of what I'm feeling without being able to actually feel it. I cannot scream until my throat hurts or break a window with my fist until my hand bleeds, or pull my hair out in clumps until the pain in my scalp overcomes the one in my heart.

I'm staring at myself, at the 'live' Mia now, lying in her hospital bed. I feel a burst of fury. If I could slap my own lifeless face, I would.

Instead, I sit down in the chair and close my eyes, wishing it all away. Except I can't. I can't concentrate because there's suddenly so much noise. My monitors are blipping and chirping and two nurses are racing toward me.

'Her BP and pulse ox are dropping,' one yells.

'She's tachycardic,' the other yells. 'What happened?'

'Code blue, code blue in Trauma,' blares the PA.

Soon the nurses are joined by a bleary-eyed doctor, rubbing the sleep out of his eyes, which are ringed by deep circles. He yanks down the covers and lifts my hospital gown. I'm naked from the waist down, but no one notices these things here. He puts his hands on my belly, which is swollen and hard. His eyes widen and then narrow into slits. 'Abdomen's rigid,' he says angrily. 'We need to do an ultrasound.'

Nurse Ramirez runs to a back room and then wheels out what looks like a portable laptop with a long white attachment. She squirts some jelly on my stomach, and the doctor runs the attachment over my stomach.

'Damn. Full of fluid,' he says. 'Patient had surgery this afternoon?'

'A splenectomy,' Nurse Ramirez replies.

'Could be a missed blood vessel that wasn't cauterized,' the doctor says. 'Or a slow leak from a perforated bowel. Car accident, right?'

'Yes. Patient was medevacced in this morning.'

The doctor flips through my chart. 'Doctor Sorensen was her surgeon. He's still on call. Page him, get her to the OR. We need to get inside and find out what's leaking, and why, before she drops any further. Jesus, brain contusions, collapsed lung. This kid's a train wreck.'

Nurse Ramirez shoots the doctor a dirty look, as if he had just insulted me.

'Miss Ramirez,' the grumpy nurse at the desk scolds. 'You have patients of your own to deal with. Let's get this young woman intubated and transferred to the OR. That will do her more good than all this dilly-dallying around!'

The nurses work rapidly to detach the monitors and catheters and run another tube down my throat. A pair of orderlies rush in with a gurney and heave me onto it. I'm still naked from the waist down as they hustle me out, but right before I reach the back door, Nurse Ramirez calls, 'Wait!' and then gently closes the hospital gown around my legs. She taps me three times on the forehead with her fingers, like it's some kind of Morse-code message. And then I'm gone into the maze of hallways leading toward the OR for another round of cutting, but this time I don't follow myself. This time I stay behind in the ICU.

I am starting to get it now. I mean, I don't totally fully understand. It's not like I somehow commanded a blood vessel to pop open and start leaking into my stomach. It's not like I wished for another surgery. But Teddy is gone. Mom and Dad are gone. This morning I went for a drive with my family. And now I am here, as alone as I've ever been. I am seventeen years old. This is not how it's supposed to be. This is not how my life is supposed to turn out.

In the quiet corner of the ICU I start to really think about the bitter things I've managed to ignore so far today. What would it be like if I stay? What would it feel like to wake up an orphan? To never smell Dad smoke a pipe? To never stand next to Mom quietly talking as we do the dishes? To never read Teddy another chapter of *Harry Potter*? To stay without them?

I'm not sure this is a world I belong in anymore. I'm not sure that I want to wake up.

*

I've only ever been to one funeral in my life and it was for someone I hardly knew.

I might have gone to Great Aunt Glo's funeral after she died of acute pancreatitis. Except her will was very specific about her final wishes. No traditional service, no burial in the family plot. Instead, she wanted to be cremated and have her ashes scattered in a sacred Native American ceremony somewhere in the Sierra Nevada Mountains. Gran was pretty annoyed by that, by Aunt Glo in general, who Gran said was always trying to call attention to how different she was, even after she was dead. Gran ended up boycotting the ash scattering, and if she wasn't going, there was no reason for the rest of us to.

Peter Hellman, my trombonist friend from conservatory camp, he died two years ago, but I didn't find out until I returned to camp and he wasn't there. Few of us had known that he'd had lymphoma. That was the funny thing about conservatory camp; you got so close with the people over the summer, but it was some unwritten rule that you didn't keep in touch during the rest of the year. We were summer friends. Anyhow, we had a memorial concert at camp in Peter's honor, but it wasn't really a funeral.

Kerry Gifford was a musician in town, one of Mom and Dad's people. Unlike Dad and Henry, who as they got older and had families became less music performers than music connoisseurs, Kerry stayed single and stayed faithful to his first love: playing music. He was in three bands and he earned his living doing the sound at a local club, an ideal setup because at least one of his bands seemed to play there every week, so he just had to hop up on the stage and let someone take the controls for his set, though sometimes you'd see him jumping down in the middle of a set to adjust the monitors himself. I had known Kerry when I was little and would go to shows with Mom and Dad and then I sort of re-met him when Adam and I got together and I started going to shows again.

He was at work one night, doing the sound for a Portland band called Clod, when he just keeled over on the soundboard. He was dead by the time the ambulance got there. A freak brain aneurysm.

Kerry's death caused an uproar in our town. He was kind of a fixture around here, an outspoken guy with a big personality and this mass of wild white-boy dreadlocks. And he was young, only thirty-two. Everyone we knew was planning on going to his funeral, which was being held in the town where he grew up, in the mountains a couple of hours drive away. Mom and Dad were going, of course, and so was Adam. So even though I felt a little bit like an impostor crashing someone's death day, I decided to go along. Teddy stayed with Gran and Gramps.

We caravanned to Kerry's hometown with a bunch of people, squeezing into a car with Henry and Willow, who was so pregnant the seat belt wouldn't fit over her bump. Everyone took turns telling funny stories about Kerry. Kerry the avowed left-winger who decided to protest the Iraq war by getting a bunch of guys to dress up in drag and go down to the local army recruiting office to enlist. Kerry the atheist curmudgeon, who hated how commercialized Christmas had become and so threw an annual Merry Anti-Christmas Celebration at the club, where he held a contest for which band could play the most distorted versions of Christmas carols. Then he invited everyone to throw all their crappy presents into a big pile in the middle of the club. And contrary to local lore, Kerry did not burn the stuff in a bonfire; Dad told me that he donated it to St Vincent de Paul.

As everyone talked about Kerry, the mood in the car was fizzy and fun, like we were going to the circus, not a funeral. But it seemed right, it seemed true to Kerry, who was always overflowing with frenetic energy.

The funeral, though, was the opposite. It was horribly depressing – and not just because it was for someone who'd died tragically young and for no particular reason aside from some bad arterial luck. It was held in a huge church, which seemed strange considering Kerry was an outspoken atheist, but that part I could understand. I mean where else do you have a funeral? The problem was the service itself. It was obvious that the pastor had never even met Kerry because when he talked about him, it was generic, about what a kind heart Kerry had and how even though it was sad that he was gone, he was getting his 'heavenly reward'.

And instead of having eulogies from his bandmates or the people in town who he'd spent the last fifteen years with, some uncle from Boise got up and talked about teaching Kerry how to ride a bike when he was six, like learning to ride a bike was the defining moment in Kerry's life. He concluded by reassuring us that Kerry was walking with Jesus now. I could see my mom getting red when he said that, and I started to get a little worried that she might say something. We went to church sometimes, so it's not like Mom had anything against religion, but Kerry totally did and Mom was ferociously protective of the people she loved, so much that she took insults upon them personally. Her friends sometimes called her Mama Bear for this reason. Steam was practically blowing out of Mom's ears by the time the service ended with a rousing rendition of Bette Midler's 'Wind Beneath My Wings'.

'It's a good thing Kerry's dead, because that funeral would've sent him over the edge,' Henry said. After the church service, we'd decided to skip the formal luncheon and had gone to a diner.

'"Wind Beneath My Wings"?' Adam asked, absent-mindedly taking my hand into his and blowing on it, which is what he did to warm my perpetually cold fingers. 'What's wrong with "Amazing Grace"? It's still traditional—'

'But doesn't make you want to puke,' Henry interjected.

'Or better yet, 'Three Little Birds' by Bob Marley. That would have been a more Kerry-worthy song. Something to toast the guy he was.'

'That funeral wasn't about celebrating Kerry's life,' Mom growled, yanking at her scarf. 'It was about repudiating it. It was like they killed him all over again.'

Dad put a calming hand over Mom's clenched fist. 'Now come on. It was just a song.'

'It wasn't just a song,' Mom said, snatching her hand away. 'It was what it represented. That whole charade back there. You of all people should understand.'

Dad shrugged and smiled sadly. 'Maybe I should. But I can't be angry with his family. I imagine this funeral was their way of reclaiming their son.'

'Please,' Mom said, shaking her head. 'If they wanted to claim their son, why didn't they respect the life he chose to live? How come they never came to visit? Or supported his music?'

'We don't know what they thought about all that,' Dad replied. 'Let's not judge too harshly. It has to be heart-breaking to bury your child.'

'I can't believe you're making excuses for them,' Mom exclaimed.

'I'm not. I just think you might be reading too much into a musical selection.'

'And I think you're confusing being empathetic with being a pushover!'

Dad's wince was barely visible, but it was enough to make Adam squeeze my hand and Henry and Willow exchange a look. Henry jumped in, to Dad's rescue, I think. 'It's different for you, with your parents,' he told Dad. 'I mean they're old-fashioned but they always were into what you did, and even in your wildest days, you were always a good son, a good father. Always home for Sunday dinner.'

Mom guffawed, as if Henry's statement had proven her point. We all turned to her, and our shocked expressions seemed to snap her out of her rant. 'Clearly I'm just emotional right now,' she said. Dad seemed to understand that was as much an apology as he was going to get right now. He covered her hand with his and this time she didn't snatch it away.

Dad paused, hesitating before speaking. 'I just think that funerals are a lot like death itself. You can have your wishes, your plans, but at the end of the day, it's out of your control.'

'No way,' Henry said. 'Not if you make your wishes known to the right people.' He turned to Willow and spoke to the bump in her belly. 'So listen up, family. At my funeral no one is allowed to wear black. And for music, I want something poppy and old-school, like Mr T Experience.' He looked up at Willow. 'Got that?'

'Mr T Experience. I'll make sure of it.'

'Thanks, and what about you, honey?' he asked her.

Without missing a beat, Willow said: 'Play "P.S. You Rock My World" by the Eels. And I want one of those green funerals where they bury you in the ground under a tree. So the funeral itself would be in nature. And no flowers. I mean, give me all the peonies you want when I'm alive, but once I'm dead, better to give donations on my behalf to a good charity like Doctors Without Borders.'

'You've got all the details figured out,' Adam said. 'Is that a nurse thing?'

Willow shrugged.

'According to Kim, that means you're deep,' I said. 'She says that the world is divided into the people who imagine their own funerals and the people who don't, and that smart and artistic people naturally fall into the former category.'

'So which are you?' Adam asked me.

'I'd want Mozart's Requiem,' I said. I turned to Mom and Dad. 'Don't worry, I'm not suicidal or anything.'

'Please,' Mom said, her mood lightening as she stirred her coffee. 'When I was growing up I'd have elaborate fantasies about my funeral. My deadbeat father and all the friends who'd wronged me would weep over my casket, which would be red, naturally, and they'd play James Taylor.'

'Let me guess,' Willow said. ' "Fire and Rain"?'

Mom nodded and she and Willow started laughing and soon everyone at the table was cracking up so hard that tears ran down our faces. And then we were crying, even me, who didn't know Kerry all that well. Crying and laughing, laughing and crying.

'So what now?' Adam asked Mom when we'd calmed down. 'Still harbor a soft spot for Mr Taylor?'

Mom stopped and blinked hard, which is what she does when she's thinking about something. Then she reached over to stroke Dad's cheek, a rare demonstration of PDA. 'In my ideal scenario, my big-hearted pushover husband and I die quickly and simultaneously when we're ninety-two years old. I'm not sure how. Maybe we're on a safari in Africa – 'cause in the future, we're rich; hey, it's my fantasy – and we come down with some exotic sickness and go to sleep one night feeling fine and then never wake up. And no James Taylor. Mia plays at our funeral. If, that is, we can tear her away from the New York Philharmonic.'

Dad was wrong. It's true you might not get to control your funeral, but sometimes you do get to choose your death. And I can't help thinking that part of Mom's wish *did* come true. She went with Dad. But I won't be playing at her funeral. It's possible that her funeral will also be mine.

There's something comforting in that. To go down as a family. No one left behind. That said, I can't help thinking Mom would not be happy about this. In fact, Mama Bear would be absolutely furious with the way events are unfolding today.

2:48 a.m.

I'm back where I started. Back in the ICU. My body, that is. *I've* been sitting here all along, too tired to move. I wish I could go to sleep. I wish there was some kind of anesthesia for *me*, or at least something to make the world shut up. I want to be like my body, quiet and lifeless, putty in someone else's hands. I don't have the energy for this decision. I don't want this anymore. I say it out loud. *I don't want this*. I look around the ICU, feeling kind of ridiculous. I doubt all the other messed-up people in the ward are exactly thrilled to be here, either.

My body wasn't gone from the ICU for too long. A few hours for surgery. Some time in the recovery room. I don't know exactly what's happened to me, and for the first time today, I don't really care. I shouldn't have to care. I shouldn't have to work this hard. I realize now that dying is easy. Living is hard.

I'm back on the ventilator, and once again there's tape over my eyes. I still don't understand the tape. Are the doctors afraid that I'll wake up mid-surgery and be horrified by the scalpels or blood? As if those things could faze me now. Two nurses, the one assigned to me and Nurse Ramirez, come over to my bed and check all my monitors. They call out a chorus of numbers that are as familiar to me now as my own name: BP, pulse ox, respiratory rate. Nurse Ramirez looks like an entirely different person from the one who arrived here yesterday afternoon. The make-up has all rubbed off and her hair is flat. She looks like she could sleep standing up. Her shift must be over soon. I'll miss her but I'm glad she'll be able to get away from me, from this place. I'd like to get away, too. I think I will. I think it's just a matter of time – of figuring out how to let go.

I haven't been back in my bed fifteen minutes when Willow shows up. She marches through the double doors and goes to speak to the one nurse behind the desk. I don't hear what she says, but I hear her tone: it's polite, soft-spoken, but leaving no room for questions. When she leaves the room a few minutes later, there's a change in the air. Willow's in charge now. The grumpy nurse at first looks pissed off, like *Who is this woman to tell me what to do?* But then she seems to resign, to throw her hands up in surrender. It's been a crazy night. The shift is almost over.

Why bother? Soon, me and all of my noisy, pushy visitors will be somebody else's problem.

Five minutes later, Willow is back, bringing Gran and Gramps with her. Willow has worked all day and now she is here all night. I know she doesn't get enough sleep on a good day. I used to hear Mom give her tips for getting the baby to sleep through the night.

I'm not sure who looks worse, me or Gramps. His cheeks are sallow, his skin looks gray and papery, and his eyes are bloodshot. Gran, on the other hand, looks just like Gran. No sign of wear and tear on her. It's like exhaustion wouldn't dare mess with her. She bustles right over to my bed.

'You've sure got us on a roller-coaster ride today,' Gran says lightly. 'Your mom always said she couldn't believe what an easy girl you were and I remember telling her, 'Just wait until she hits puberty.' But you proved me wrong. Even then you were such a breeze. Never gave us any trouble. Never the kind of girl to make my heart race in fear. You made up for a lifetime of that today.'

'Now, now,' Gramps says, putting a hand on her shoulder.

'Oh, I'm only kidding. Mia would appreciate it. She's got a sense of humor, no matter how serious she sometimes seems. A wicked sense of humor, this one.'

Gran pulls the chair up next to my bed and starts

combing through my hair with her fingers. Someone has rinsed it out, so, while it's not exactly clean, it's not caked with blood, either. Gran starts untangling my bangs, which are about chin length. I'm forever cutting bangs, then growing them. It's about as radical a makeover as I can give myself. She works her way down, pulling the hair out from under the pillow so it streams down my chest, hiding some of the lines and tubes connected to me. 'There, much better,' she says. 'You know, I went outside for a walk today and you'll never guess what I saw? A crossbill. In Portland in February. Now, that's unusual. I think it's Glo. She always had a soft spot for you. Said you reminded her of your father, and she adored him. When he cut his first crazy Mohawk hairdo, she practically threw him a party. She loved that he was rebellious, so different. Little did she know your father couldn't stand her. She came to visit us once when your dad was around five or six, and she had this ratty mink coat with her. This was before she got all into the animal rights and crystals and the like. The coat smelled terrible, like mothballs, like the old linens we kept in a trunk in the attic, and your father took to calling her 'Auntie Trunk Smell'. She never knew that. But she loved that he'd rebelled against us, or so she thought, and she thought it was something that you rebelled all over again by becoming a classical musician. Though much as I tried to tell her that it wasn't the way it was, she didn't care. She had her own ideas about things; I suppose we all do.'

Gran twitters on for another five minutes, filling me in on mundane news: Heather has decided she wants to become a librarian. My cousin Matthew bought a motorcycle and my aunt Patricia is not pleased about that. I've heard her keep up a running stream of commentary like this for hours while she's cooking dinner or potting orchids. And listening to her now, I can almost picture us in her greenhouse, where even in winter, the air is always warm and humid and smells musty and earthy like soil with the slightest tinge of manure. Gran hand-collects cowshit, 'cow-patties', she calls them, and mixes them in with mulch to make her own fertilizer. Gramps thinks she should patent the recipe and sell it because she uses it on her orchids, which are always winning awards.

I try to meditate on the sound of Gran's voice, to be carried away by her happy babble. Sometimes I can almost fall asleep while sitting on the bar stool at her kitchen counter and listening to her, and I wonder if I could do that here today. Sleep would be so welcome. A warm blanket of black to erase everything else. Sleep without dreams. I've heard people talk about the sleep of the dead. Is that what death would feel like? The nicest, warmest, heaviest never-ending nap? If that's what it's like, I wouldn't mind.

If that's what dying is like, I wouldn't mind that at all.

I jerk myself up, a panic destroying whatever calm listening to Gran had offered. I am still not entirely clear on the particulars here, but I do know that once I fully commit to going, I'll go. But I'm not ready. Not yet. I don't know why, but I'm not. And I'm a little scared that if I accidentally think, I wouldn't mind an endless nap, it will happen and be irreversible, like the way my grandparents used to warn me that if I made a funny face as the clock struck noon, it would remain like that for ever.

I wonder if every dying person gets to decide whether they stay or go. It seems unlikely. After all, this hospital is full of people having poisonous chemicals pumped into their veins or submitting to horrible operations all so they can stay, but some of them will die anyway.

Did Mom and Dad decide? It hardly seems like there would have been time for them to make such a momentous decision, and I can't imagine them choosing to leave me behind. And what about Teddy? Did he want to go with Mom and Dad? Did he know that I was still here? Even if he did, I wouldn't blame him for choosing to go without me. He's little. He was probably scared. I suddenly picture him alone and frightened, and for the first time in my life, I hope that Gran is right about the angels. I pray they were all too busy comforting Teddy to worry about me.

This is all too much for a seventeen-year-old girl to have to decide. Why can't someone else decide this for me? Why can't I get a death proxy?

Gran is gone. Willow is gone. The ICU is tranquil. I close my eyes. When I open them again, Gramps is there. He's crying. He's not making any noise, but tears are cascading down his cheeks, wetting his entire face. I've never seen anyone cry like this. Quiet but gushing, a faucet behind his eyes mysteriously turned on. The tears fall onto my blanket, onto my freshly combed hair. *Plink. Plink. Plink.*

Gramps doesn't wipe his face or blow his nose. He just lets the tears fall where they may. And when the well of grief is momentarily dry, he steps forward and kisses me on the forehead. He looks like he's about to leave, but then he doubles back to my bedside, bends so his face is level with my ear, and whispers into it.

'It's OK,' he tells me. 'If you want to go. Everyone wants you to stay. *I* want you to stay more than I've ever wanted anything in my life.' His voice cracks with emotion. He stops, clears his throat, takes a breath, and continues. 'But that's what I want and I could see why it might not be what you want. So I just wanted to tell you that I understand if you go. It's OK if you have to leave us. It's OK if you want to stop fighting.'

For the first time since I realized that Teddy was gone, too, I feel something unclench. I feel myself breathe. I know that Gramps can't be that death proxy I'd hoped for. He won't unplug my breathing tube or overdose me with morphine or anything like that. But this is the first time today that anyone has acknowledged what I have lost. I know that the social worker warned Gran and Gramps not to upset me, but Gramps's recognition, and the permission he just offered me – it feels like a gift.

Gramps doesn't leave me. He slumps back into the chair. It's quiet now. So quiet that you can almost hear other people's dreams. So quiet that you can almost hear me tell Gramps, 'Thank you.'

*

When Mom had Teddy, Dad was still playing drums in the same band he'd been in since college. They'd released a couple of CDs; they'd gone on a tour every summer. The band was by no means big, but they had a following in the Northwest and in various college towns between here and Chicago. And, weirdly, they had a bunch of fans in Japan. The band was always getting letters from Japanese teenagers begging them to come play, and offering up their homes as crash pads. Dad was always saying that if they went, he'd take me and Mom. Mom and I even learned a few words of Japanese just in case. *Konnichiwa. Arigatou.* It never panned out, though.

After Mom announced she was pregnant with Teddy, the first sign that changes were afoot was when Dad went and got himself a learner's permit. At age thirty-three. He tried letting Mom teach him to drive, but she was too impatient, he said. Dad was too sensitive to criticism, Mom said. So Gramps took Dad out along the empty country lanes in his pickup truck, just like he'd done with the rest of Dad's siblings – except they'd all learned to drive when they were sixteen.

Next up was the wardrobe change, but it wasn't something any of us noticed right away. It wasn't like one day he stripped off the tight black jeans and band tees in exchange for suits. It was more subtle. First the band tees went out in the window in favor of button-up 1950s rayon numbers, which he dug up at the Goodwill until they started getting trendy and he had to buy them from the fancy vintage-clothing shop. Then the jeans went in the bin, except for one pair of impeccable, dark blue Levi's, which Dad ironed and wore on weekends. Most days he wore neat, flat-front cuffed trousers. But when, a few weeks after Teddy was born, Dad gave away his leather jacket – his prized beat-up motorcycle jacket with the fuzzy leopard belt – we finally realized that a major transformation was under way.

'Dude, you cannot be serious,' Henry said when Dad handed him the jacket. 'You've been wearing this thing since you were a kid. It even smells like you.'

Dad shrugged, ending the conversation. Then he went to pick up Teddy, who was squalling from his bassinet.

A few months later, Dad announced he was leaving the band. Mom told him not to do it for her sake. She said it was OK to keep playing as long as he didn't take off on month-long tours, leaving her alone with two kids. Dad said not to worry, he wasn't quitting for her.

Dad's other bandmates took his decision in stride, but Henry was devastated. He tried to talk him out of it. Promised they'd only play in town. Wouldn't have to tour. Ever be gone overnight. 'We can even start playing shows in suits. We'll look like the Rat Pack. Do Sinatra covers. Come on, man,' Henry reasoned.

When Dad refused to reconsider, he and Henry had a huge blowout. Henry was furious with Dad for unilaterally quitting the band, especially since Mom had said he could still play shows. Dad told Henry that he was sorry, but he'd made his decision. By this time, he'd already filled out his applications for grad school. He was going to be a teacher now. No more dicking around. 'One day you'll understand,' Dad told Henry.

'The fuck I will,' Henry shot back.

Henry didn't speak to Dad for a few months after that. Willow would drop by from time to time, to play peacemaker. She'd explain to Dad that Henry was just sorting some stuff out. 'Give him time,' she said, and Dad would pretend to not be hurt. Then she and Mom would drink coffee in the kitchen and exchange knowing smiles that seemed to say: *Men are such boys.*

Henry eventually resurfaced, but he didn't apologize to Dad, not right away, anyhow. Years later, shortly after his daughter was born, Henry called our house one night in tears. 'I get it now,' he told Dad.

Strangely enough, in some ways Gramps seemed as upset with Dad's metamorphosis as Henry had been. You would have thought he would love the new Dad. On the surface, he and Gran seem so old-school, it's like a time warp. They don't use computers or watch cable TV, and they never curse and have this thing about them that makes you want to be polite. Mom, who swore like a prison guard, never cursed around Gran and Gramps. It was like no one wanted to disappoint them.

Gran got a kick out of Dad's stylistic transformation. 'Had I known that all that stuff was going to come back in style, I would've saved Gramps's old suits,' Gran said one Sunday afternoon when we'd stopped by for lunch and Dad pulled off a trench coat to reveal a pair of wool gabardine trousers and a 1950s cardigan.

'It hasn't come back into style. *Punk* has come into style, so I think this is your son's way of rebelling all over again,' Mom said with a smirk. 'Whose daddy's a rebel? Is your daddy a rebel?' Mom baby-talked as Teddy gurgled in delight.

'Well, he sure does look dapper,' Gran said. 'Don't you think?' she said, turning to Gramps.

Gramps shrugged. 'He always looks good to me. All my children and grandchildren do.' But he looked pained as he said it.

Later that afternoon, I went outside with Gramps to help him collect firewood. He needed to split some more logs, so I watched him take an ax to a bunch of dried alder.

'Gramps, don't you like Dad's new clothes?' I asked.

Gramps halted the ax in midair. Then he set it down gently next to the bench I was sitting on. 'I like his clothes just fine, Mia,' he said.

'But you looked so sad in there when Gran was talking about it.'

Gramps shook his head. 'Don't miss a thing, do you? Even at ten years old.'

'It's not easy to miss. When you feel sad, you look sad.'

'I'm not sad. Your father seems happy and I think he'll make a good teacher. Those are some lucky kids who get to read *The Great Gatsby* with your dad. I'll just miss the music.'

'Music? You never go to Dad's shows.'

'I've got bad ears. From the war. The noise hurts.'

'You should wear headphones. Mom makes me do that. Earplugs just fall out.'

'Maybe I'll try that. But I've always listened to your dad's music. At low volume. I'll admit, I don't much care for all that electric guitar. Not my cup of tea. But I still admired the music. The words, especially. When he was about your age, your father used to come up with these great stories. He'd sit down at his little table and write them down, then give them to Gran to type up, then he'd draw pictures. Funny stories about animals, but real and smart. Always reminded me of that book about the spider and the pig – what's it called?'

'*Charlotte's Web*?'

'That's the one. I always thought your dad would grow up

to be a writer. And in a way, I always felt like he did. The words he writes to his music, they're poetry. You ever listen carefully to the things he says?'

I shook my head, suddenly ashamed. I hadn't even realized that Dad wrote lyrics. He didn't sing so I just assumed that the people in front of the microphones wrote the words. But I *had* seen him sit at the kitchen table with a guitar and a notepad a hundred times. I'd just never put it together.

That night when we got home, I went up to my room with Dad's CDs and a Discman. I checked the liner notes to see which songs Dad had written and then I painstakingly copied down all the lyrics. It was only after I saw them scrawled in my science lab book that I saw what Gramps meant. Dad's lyrics were not just rhymes. They were something else. There was one song in particular called 'Waiting for Vengeance' that I listened to and read over and over until I had it memorized. It was on the second album, and it was the only slow song they ever did; it sounded almost country, probably from Henry's brief infatuation with hillbilly punk. I listened to it so much that I started singing it to myself without even realizing it.

'Well, what is this?

What am I coming to?

And beyond that, what am I gonna do?

Now there's blankness

Where once your eyes held the light

But that was so long ago

That was last night

'Well, what was that?

What's that sound that I hear?

It's just my lifetime

It's whistling past my ear

And when I look back

Everything seems smaller than life

The way it's been for so long

Since last night

'Now I'm leaving

Any moment I'll be gone

I think you'll notice

I think you'll wonder what went wrong

I'm not choosing

But I'm running out of fight

And this was decided so long ago

It was last night . . .'

'What are you singing, Mia?' Dad asked me, catching me serenading Teddy as I pushed him around the kitchen in his stroller in a vain attempt to get him to nap.

'Your song,' I said sheepishly, suddenly feeling like I'd maybe illegally trespassed into Dad's private territory. Was it wrong to go around singing other people's music without their permission?

But Dad looked delighted. 'My Mia's singing "Waiting for Vengeance" to my Teddy. What do you think about that?' He leaned over to muss my hair and to tickle Teddy on his chubby cheek. 'Well, don't let me stop you. Keep going. I'll take over this part,' he said, taking the stroller.

I felt embarrassed to sing in front of him now, so I just sort of mumbled along, but then Dad joined in and we sang softly together until Teddy fell asleep. Then he put a finger over his lips and gestured for me to follow him into the living room.

'Want to play some chess?' he asked. He was always trying to teach me to play, but I thought it was too much work for a supposed game.

'How about checkers?' I asked.

'Sure.'

We played in silence. When it was Dad's move, I'd steal looks at him in his button-down shirt, trying to remember the fast-fading picture of the guy with peroxided hair and a leather jacket.

'Dad?'

'Hmm.'

'Can I ask you a question?'

'Always.'

'Are you sad that you aren't in a band anymore?'

'Nope,' he said.

'Not even a little bit?'

Dad's gray eyes met mine. 'What brought this all on?'

'I was talking to Gramps.'

'Oh, I see.'

'You do?'

Dad nodded. 'Gramps thinks that he somehow exerted pressure on me to change my life.'

'Well, did he?'

'I suppose in an indirect way he did. By being who he is, by showing me what a father is.'

'But you were a good dad when you played in a band. The *best* dad. I wouldn't want you to give that up for me,' I said, feeling suddenly choked up. 'And I don't think Teddy would, either.'

Dad smiled and patted my hand. 'Mia Oh-My-Uh. I'm not giving anything up. It's not an either-or proposition. Teaching or music. Jeans or suits. Music will always be a part of my life.'

'But you quit the band! Gave up dressing punk!'

Dad sighed. 'It wasn't hard to do. I'd played that part of my life out. It was time. I didn't even think twice about it, in spite of what Gramps or Henry might think. Sometimes you make choices in life and sometimes choices make you. Does that make any sense?'

I thought about the cello. How sometimes I didn't understand why I'd been drawn to it, how some days it seemed as if the instrument had chosen me. I nodded, smiled, and returned my attention to the game. 'King me,' I said.

4:57 a.m.

I can't stop thinking about 'Waiting for Vengeance.' It's been years since I've listened to or thought of that song, but after Gramps left my bedside, I've been singing it to myself over and over. Dad wrote the song ages ago, but now it feels like he wrote it yesterday. Like he wrote it from wherever he is. Like there's a secret message in it for me. How else to explain those lyrics? *I'm not choosing. But I'm running out of fight.*

What does it mean? Is it supposed to be some kind of instruction? Some clue about what my parents would choose for me if they could? I try to think about it from their perspectives. I know they'd want to be with me, for us all to be together again eventually. But I have no idea if that even happens after you die, and if it does, it'll happen whether I go this morning or in seventy years. What would they want for me *now*? As soon as I pose the question, I can see Mom's pissed-off expression. She'd be livid with me for even contemplating anything *but* staying. But Dad, he understood what it meant to run out of fight. Maybe, like Gramps, he'd understand why I don't think I *can* stay.

I'm singing the song, as if buried within its lyrics are instructions, a musical road map to where I'm supposed to go and how to get there.

I'm singing and concentrating and singing and thinking so hard that I barely register Willow's return to the ICU, barely notice that she's talking to the grumpy nurse, barely recognize the steely determination in her tone.

Had I been paying attention, I might have realized that Willow was lobbying for Adam to be able to visit me. Had I been paying attention, I might have somehow got away before Willow was – as always – successful.

I don't want to see him now. I mean, of course I do. I ache to. But I know that if I see him, I'm going to lose the last wisp of peacefulness that Gramps gave me when he told me that it was OK to go. I'm trying to summon the courage to do what I have to do. And Adam will complicate things. I try to stand up to get away, but something has happened to me since I went back into surgery. I no longer have the strength to move. It takes all my effort to sit upright in my chair. I can't run away; all I can do is hide. I curl my knees into my chest and close my eyes.

I hear Nurse Ramirez talking to Willow. 'I'll take him over,' she says. And for once, the grumpy nurse doesn't order her back to her own patients.

'That was a pretty boneheaded move you pulled earlier,' I hear her tell Adam.

'I know,' Adam answers. His voice is a throaty whisper, the way it gets after a particularly screamy concert. 'I was desperate.'

'No, you were romantic,' she tells him.

'I was idiotic. They said she was doing better before. That she'd come off the ventilator. That she was getting stronger. But after I came in here that she got worse. They said her heart stopped on the operating table . . .' Adam trails off.

'And they got it started. She had a perforated bowel that was slowly leaking bile into her abdomen and it threw her organs out of whack. This kind of thing happens all the time, and it had nothing to do with you. We caught it and fixed it and that's what matters.'

'But she was doing better,' Adam whispers. He sounds so young and vulnerable, like Teddy used to sound when he got the stomach flu. 'And then I came in and she almost died.' His voice chokes into a sob. The sound of it wakes me up like a bucket of ice water dropped down my shirt. Adam thinks that *he* did this to me? No! That's beyond absurd. He's so wrong.

'And I *almost* stayed in Puerto Rico to marry a fat SOB,' the nurse snaps. 'But I didn't. And I have a different life now. *Almost* don't matter. You got to deal with the situation at hand. And she's still here.' She whips the privacy curtain around my bed. 'In you go,' she tells Adam.

I force my head up and my eyes open. Adam. God, even in this state, he is beautiful. His eyes are dipping with fatigue. He's sprouting stubble, enough of it that if we were to make out, it would make my chin raw. He is wearing his typical band uniform of a T-shirt, skinny pegged pants, and Converse, with Gramps's plaid scarf draped over his shoulders.

When he first sees me, he blanches, like I'm some hideous Creature from the Black Lagoon. I do look pretty bad, hooked back up to the ventilator and a dozen other tubes, the dressing from my latest surgery seeping blood. But after a moment, Adam exhales loudly and then he's just Adam again. He searches around, like he's dropped something and then finds what he's looking for: my hand.

'Jesus, Mia, your hands are freezing.' He squats down, takes my right hand into his, and careful to not bump into my tubes and wires, draws his mouth to them, blowing warm air into the shelter he's created. 'You and your crazy hands.' Adam is always amazed at how even in middle of summer, even after the sweatiest of encounters, my hands stay cold. I tell him it's bad circulation but he doesn't buy it because my feet are usually warm. He says I have bionic hands, that this is why I'm such a good cello player.

I watch him warm my hands as he has done a thousand times before. I think of the first time he did it, at school, sitting on the lawn, as if it were the most natural thing in the world. I also remember the first time he did it in front of my parents. We were all sitting on the porch on Christmas Eve, drinking cider. It was freezing outside. Adam grabbed my hands and blew on them. Teddy giggled. Mom and Dad didn't say anything, just exchanged a quick look, something private that passed between them and then Mom smiled ruefully at us.

I wonder if I tried, if I could feel him touching me. If I were to lie down on top of myself in the bed, would I become one with my body again? Would I feel him then? If I reached out my ghostly hand to his, would he feel me? Would he warm the hands he cannot see?

Adam drops my hand and steps forward to look at me. He is standing so close that I can almost smell him and I'm overpowered by the need to touch him. It's basic, primal, and all-consuming the way a baby needs its mother's breast. Even though I know, if we touch, a new tug-of-war – one that will be even more painful than the quiet one Adam and I have been waging these past few months – will begin.

Adam is mumbling something now. In a low voice. Over and over he is saying: please. *Please. Please. Please. Please. Please. Please. Please. Please. Please.* Finally, he stops and looks at my face. 'Please, Mia,' he implores. 'Don't make me write a song.'

*

I'd never expected to fall in love. I was never the kind of girl who had crushes on rock stars or fantasies about marrying Brad Pitt. I sort of vaguely knew that one day I'd probably have boyfriends (in college, if Kim's prediction was anything to go by) and get married. I wasn't totally immune to the charms of the opposite sex, but I wasn't one of those romantic, swoony girls who had pink fluffy daydreams about falling in love.

Even as I was falling in love – full throttle, intense, can't-erase-that-goofy-smile love – I didn't really register what was happening. When I was with Adam, at least after those first few awkward weeks, I felt so good that I didn't bother thinking about what was going on with me, with us. It just felt normal and right, like slipping into a hot bubble bath.

Which isn't to say we didn't fight. We argued over lots of stuff: him not being nice enough to Kim, me being antisocial at shows, how fast he drove, how I stole the covers. I got upset because he never wrote any songs about me. He claimed he wasn't good with sappy love songs: 'If you want a song, you'll have to cheat on me or something,' he said, knowing full well that wasn't going to happen.

This past fall, though, Adam and I started to have a different kind of fight. It wasn't even a fight, really. We didn't shout. We barely even argued, but a snake of tension quietly slithered into our lives. And it seemed like it all started with my Juilliard audition.

'So did you knock them dead?' Adam asked me when I got back. 'They gonna let you in with a full scholarship?'

I had a feeling that they were going to let me in, at least – even before I told Professor Christie about the one judge's 'long time since we've had an Oregon country girl' comment, even before she hyperventilated because she was so convinced this was a tacit promise of admission. Something had happened to my playing in that audition; I had broken through some invisible barrier and could finally play the pieces like I heard them being played in my head, and the result had been something transcendent: the mental and physical, the technical and emotional sides of my abilities all finally blending. Then, on the drive home, as Gramps and I were approaching the California-Oregon border, I just had this sudden flash – a vision of me lugging a cello through New York City. And it was like I *knew*, and that certainty planted itself in my belly like a warm secret. I'm not the kind of person who's prone to premonitions or overconfidence, so I suspected that there was more to my flash than magical thinking.

'I did OK,' I told Adam, and as I said it, I realized that I'd just straight-out lied to him for the first time, and that this was different from all the lying by omission I'd been doing before.

I had neglected to tell Adam that I was applying to Juilliard in the first place, which was actually harder than it sounded. Before I sent in my application, I had to practice every spare moment with Professor Christie to fine-tune the Shostakovich concerto and the two Bach suites. When Adam asked me why I was so busy, I gave purposely vague excuses about learning tough new pieces. I justified this to myself because it was technically true. And then Professor Christie arranged for me to have a recording session at the university so I could submit a high-quality CD to Juilliard. I had to be at the studio at seven in the morning on a Sunday and the night before I'd pretended to be feeling out of sorts and told Adam he probably shouldn't stay over. I'd justified that fib, too. I was feeling out of sorts because I was so nervous. So, it wasn't a real lie. And besides, I thought, there was no point in making a big fuss about it. I hadn't told Kim, either, so it wasn't like Adam was getting special deception treatment.

But after I told him I'd only done OK at the audition, I had the feeling that I was wading into quicksand, and that if I took one more step, there'd be no extricating myself and I'd sink until I suffocated. So I took a deep breath and heaved myself back onto solid ground. 'Actually, that's not true,' I told Adam. 'I did really well. I played better than I ever have in my life. It was like I was possessed.'

Adam's first reaction was to smile with pride. 'I wish I could've seen that.' But then his eyes clouded over and his lips fell into a frown. 'Why'd you downplay it?' he asked. 'Why didn't you call me after the audition to brag?'

'I don't know,' I said.

'Well, this is great news,' Adam said, trying to mask his hurt. 'We should be celebrating.'

'OK, let's celebrate,' I said, with a forced gaiety. 'We can go to Portland Saturday. Go to the Japanese Gardens and go out for dinner at Beau Thai.'

Adam grimaced. 'I can't. We're playing in Olympia and Seattle this weekend. Mini-tour. Remember? I'd love for you to come, but I don't know if that's really a celebration for you. But I'll be back Sunday late afternoon. I can meet you in Portland Sunday night if you want.'

'I can't. I'm playing in a string quartet at some professor's house. What about next weekend?'

Adam looked pained. 'We're in the studio the next couple weekends, but we can go out during the week somewhere. Around here. To the Mexican place?'

'Sure. The Mexican place,' I said.

Two minutes before, I hadn't even wanted to celebrate, but now I was feeling dejected and insulted at being relegated to a midweek dinner at the same place we always went to.

When Adam graduated from high school last spring and moved out of his parents' place and into the House of Rock, I hadn't expected much to change. He'd still live nearby. We'd still see each other all the time. I'd miss our little powwows in the music wing, but I would also be relieved to have our relationship out from under the microscope of high school.

But things had changed when Adam moved into the House of Rock and started college, though not for the reasons I'd thought they would. At the beginning of the fall, just as Adam was getting used to college life, things suddenly started heating up with Shooting Star. The band was offered a record deal with a medium-size label based in Seattle and now were busy in the studio recording. They were also playing more shows, to larger and larger crowds, almost every weekend. Things were so hectic that Adam had dropped half his course load and was going to college part-time, and if things kept up at this rate, he was thinking of dropping out altogether. 'There are no second chances,' he told me.

I was genuinely excited for him. I knew that Shooting Star was something special, more than just a college-town band. I hadn't minded Adam's increasing absences, especially since he made it so clear how much he minded them. But some-how, the prospect of Juilliard made things different – somehow it made me mind. Which didn't make any sense at all because if anything, it should have leveled the field. Now I had something exciting happening, too.

'We can go to Portland in a few weeks,' Adam promised. 'When all the holiday lights are up.'

'OK,' I said sullenly.

Adam sighed. 'Things are getting complicated, aren't they?'

'Yeah. Our schedules are too busy,' I said.

'That's not what I meant,' Adam said, turning my face toward his so I was looking at him in the eye.

'I know that's not what you meant,' I replied, but then a

lump lodged itself in my throat and I couldn't talk anymore.

We tried to defuse the tension, to talk about it without really talking about it, to joke-ify it. 'You know I read in *US News and World Report* that Willamette University has a good music program,' Adam told me. 'It's in Salem, which is apparently getting hipper by the moment.'

'According to who? The governor?' I replied.

'Liz found some good stuff at a vintage-clothing store there. And you know, once the vintage places come in, the hipsters aren't far behind.'

'You forget, I'm not a hipster,' I reminded him. 'But speaking of, maybe Shooting Star should move to New York. I mean, it's the heart of the punk scene. The Ramones. Blondie.' My tone was frothy and flirtatious, an Oscar-worthy performance.

'That was thirty years ago,' Adam said. 'And even if I wanted to move to New York, there's no way the rest of the band would.' He stared mournfully at his shoes and I recognized the joking part of the conversation had ended. My stomach lurched, an appetizer before the full portion of heartache I had a feeling was going to be served at some point soon.

Adam and I had never been the kind of couple to talk

about the future, about where our relationship was going, but with things suddenly so unclear, we avoided talking about *anything* that was happening more than a few weeks away, and this made our conversations as stilted and awkward as they'd been in those early weeks together before we'd found our groove. One afternoon in the fall, I spotted a beautiful 1930s silk gown in the vintage store where Dad bought his suits and I almost pointed it out to Adam and asked if he thought I should wear that to the prom, but prom was in June and maybe Adam would be on tour in June or maybe I'd be too busy getting ready for Juilliard, so I didn't say anything. Not long after that, Adam was complaining about his decrepit guitar, saying he wanted to get a vintage Gibson SG, and I offered to get it for him for his birthday. But then he said that those guitars cost thousands of dollars, and besides his birthday wasn't until September, and the way he said *September*, it was like a judge issuing a prison sentence.

A few weeks ago, we went to a New Year's Eve party together. Adam got drunk, and when midnight came, he kissed me hard. 'Promise me. Promise me you'll spend New Year's with me next year,' he whispered into my ear.

I was about to explain that even if I did go to Juilliard, I'd be home for Christmas and New Year's, but then I realized that wasn't the point. So I promised him because I wanted it to be true as much as he did. And I kissed him back so hard, like I was trying to merge our bodies through our lips.

On New Year's Day, I came home to find the rest of my family gathered in the kitchen with Henry, Willow and the baby. Dad was making breakfast: smoked-salmon hash, his specialty.

Henry shook his head when he saw me. 'Look at the kids. Seems like just yesterday that stumbling home at eight o'clock felt early. Now I'd kill just to be able to sleep until eight.'

'We didn't even make it till midnight,' Willow admitted, bouncing the baby on her lap. 'Good thing, because this little lady decided to start her new year at five-thirty.'

'I stayed up till midnight!' Teddy yelled. 'I saw the ball drop on TV at twelve. It's in New York, you know? If you move there, will you take me to see it drop in real life?' he asked.

'Sure, Teddy,' I said feigning enthusiasm. The idea of me going to New York was seeming more and more real, and though this generally filled me with a nervous, if conflicted, excitement, the image of me and Teddy hanging out together on New Year's Eve left me feeling unbearably lonely.

Mom looked at me, eyebrows arched. 'It's New Year's Day,

so I won't give you shit for coming in at this hour. But if you're hungover, you're grounded.'

'I'm not. I had one beer. I'm just tired.'

'Just tired, is it? You sure?' Mom grabbed a hold of my wrist and turned me toward her. When she saw my stricken expression, she tilted her head to the side as if to say, *You OK?* I shrugged and bit my lip to keep from losing it. Mom nodded. She handed me a cup of coffee and led me to the table. She put down a plate of hash and a thick slice of sourdough bread, and even though I couldn't imagine being hungry, my mouth watered and my stomach rumbled and I was suddenly ravenous. I ate silently, Mom watching me all the while. After everyone was done, Mom sent the rest of them into the living room to watch the Rose Parade on TV.

'Everyone out,' she ordered. 'Mia and I will do the washing up.'

As soon as everyone was gone, Mom turned to me and I just fell against her, crying and releasing all of the tension and uncertainty of the last few weeks. She stood there silently, letting me blubber all over her sweater. When I stopped, she held out the sponge. 'You wash. I'll dry. We'll talk. I always find it calming. The warm water, the soap.'

Mom picked up the dish towel and we went to work. And I told her about Adam and me. 'It was like we had this perfect year and a half,' I said. 'So perfect that I never even thought about the future. About it taking us in different directions.'

Mom's smile was both sad and knowing. 'I thought about it.'

I turned to her. She was staring straight out the window, watching a couple of sparrows bathe in a puddle. 'I remember last year when Adam came over for Christmas Eve. I told your father that you'd fallen in love too soon.'

'I know, I know. What does a dumb kid know about love?'

Mom stopped drying a skillet. 'That's not what I meant. The opposite, really. You and Adam never struck me as a "high-school" relationship,' Mom said making quote marks with her hands. 'It was nothing like the drunken roll in the back of some guy's Chevy that passed for a relationship when I was in high school. You guys seemed, still seem, in love, truly, deeply.' She sighed. 'But seventeen is an inconvenient time to be in love.'

That made me smile and made the pit in my stomach soften a little. 'Tell me about it,' I said. 'Though if we weren't both musicians, we could go to college together and be fine.'

'That's a cop-out, Mia,' Mom countered. 'All relationships are tough. Just like with music, sometimes you have harmony and other times you have cacophony. I don't have to tell you that.'

'I guess you're right.'

'And come on, music brought you two together. That's what your father and I always thought. You were both in love with music and then you fell in love with each other. It was a little like that for your dad and me. I didn't play but I listened. Luckily, I was a little older when we met.'

I'd never told Mom about what Adam had said that night after the Yo-Yo Ma concert, when I'd asked him *Why me?* How the music was totally a part of it. 'Yeah, but now I feel like it's music that's going to pull us apart.'

Mom shook her head. 'That's bullshit. Music can't do that. Life might take you down different roads. But each of you gets to decide which one to take.' She turned to face me. 'Adam's not trying to stop you going to Juilliard, is he?'

'No more than I'm trying to get him to move to New York. And it's all ridiculous anyway. I might not even go.'

'No, you might not. But you're going somewhere. I think we all get that. And the same is true for Adam.'

'At least he can go somewhere while still living here.'

Mom shrugged. 'Maybe. For now anyhow.'

I put my face in my hands and shook my head. 'What am I going to do?' I lamented. 'I feel like I'm caught in a tug-of-war.'

Mom shot me a sympathetic grimace. 'I don't know. But I do know that if you want to stay and be with him, I'd support that, though maybe I'm only saying that because I don't think you'd be able to turn down Juilliard. But I'd understand if you chose love, Adam-love, over music-love. Either way you win. And either way you lose. What can I tell you? Love's a bitch.'

Adam and I talked about it once more after that. We were at House of Rock, sitting on his futon. He was riffing about on his acoustic guitar.

'I might not get in,' I told him. 'I might wind up at school here, with you. In a way, I hope I don't get accepted so I don't have to choose.'

'If you get in, the choice is already made, isn't it?' Adam asked.

It was. I would go. It didn't mean I'd stop loving Adam or that we'd break up, but Mom and Adam were both right. I wouldn't turn down Juilliard.

Adam was silent for a minute, plinking away at his guitar so loud that I almost missed it when he said, 'I don't want to be the guy who doesn't want you to go. If the tables were turned, you'd let me go.'

'I kind of already have. In a way, you're already gone. To your own Juilliard,' I said.

'I know,' Adam said quietly. 'But I'm still here. And I'm still crazy in love with you.'

'Me, too,' I said. And then we stopped talking for a while as Adam strummed an unfamiliar melody. I asked him what he was playing.

'I'm calling it "The Girlfriend's-Going-to-Juilliard-Leaving-My-Punk-Heart-in-Shreds Blues",' he said, singing the title in an exaggeratedly twangy voice. Then he smiled that goofy shy smile that I felt like came from the truest part of him. 'I'm kidding.'

'Good,' I said.

'Sort of,' he added.

5:42 a.m.

Adam is gone. He suddenly rushed out, calling to Nurse Ramirez that he'd forgotten something important and would be back as soon as he could. He was already out the door when she told him that she was about to get off work. In fact, she just left, but not before making sure to inform the nurse who'd relieved Old Grumpy that 'the young man with the skinny pants and messy hair' is allowed to see me when he returns.

Not that it matters. Willow rules the school now. She has been marching the troops through here all morning. After Gran and Gramps and Adam, Aunt Patricia stopped by.

Then it was Aunt Diane and Uncle Greg. Then my cousins shuffled in. Willow's running to and fro, a gleam in her eye. She's up to something, but whether it's trotting out loved ones to lobby on behalf of my continuing my earthly existence or whether she's simply bringing them in to say goodbye, I can't say.

Now it's Kim's turn. Poor Kim. She looks like she slept in a Dumpster. Her hair has staged a full-scale rebellion and more of it has escaped her mangled braid than remains tucked inside. She's wearing one of what she calls her 'turd sweaters', the greenish, grayish, brownish lumpy masses her mom is always buying her. At first, Kim squints at me, as if I'm a bright, glaring light. But then it's like she adjusts to the light and decides that even though I may look like a zombie, even though there are tubes sticking out of every which orifice, even though there's blood on my thin blanket from where it's seeped through the bandages, I'm still Mia and she's still Kim. And what do Mia and Kim like to do more than anything? Talk.

Kim settles into the chair next to my bed. 'How are you doing?' she asks.

I'm not sure. I'm exhausted, but at the same time Adam's visit has left me . . . I don't know what. Agitated. Anxious. Awake, definitely awake. Though I couldn't feel it when he touched me, his presence stirred me up anyhow. I was just

191

starting to feel grateful that he was here when he booked out of here like the devil was chasing him. Adam has spent the last ten hours trying to get in to see me, and now that he finally succeeded, he left ten minutes after arriving. Maybe I scared him. Maybe he doesn't want to deal. Maybe I'm not the only chicken-shit around here. After all, I spent the last day dreaming of him coming to me, and when he finally staggered into the ICU, if I had the strength, I would've run away.

'Well, you would not believe the crazy night it's been,' Kim says. Then she starts telling me about it. About her mom's hysterics, about how she lost it in front of my relatives, who were very gracious about the whole thing. The fight they had outside the Roseland Theater in front of a bunch of punks and hipsters. When Kim shouted at her crying mother to 'pull it together and start acting like the adult around here' and then stalked off into the club leaving a shocked Mrs Schein at the curb, a group of guys in spiked leather and fluorescent hair cheered and high-fived her. She tells me about Adam, his determination to get in to see me, how after he got kicked out of the ICU, he enlisted the help of his music friends, who were not at all the snobby scenesters she'd imagined them to be. Then she told me that a bona fide rock star had come to the hospital on my behalf.

Of course, I know almost everything that Kim is telling

me, but there is no way that she'd know that. Besides, I like having her recount the day to me. I like how Kim is talking to me normally, like Gran did earlier, just jabbering on, spinning a good yarn, as if we were together on my porch, drinking coffee (or an iced caramel Frappuccino in Kim's case) and catching up.

I don't know if once you die you remember things that happened to you when you were alive. It makes a certain logical sense that you wouldn't. That being dead will feel like before you were born, which is to say, a whole lot of nothingness. Except that for me, at least, my prebirth years aren't entirely blank. Every now and again, Mom or Dad will be telling a story about something, about Dad catching his first salmon with Gramps, or Mom remembering the amazing Dead Moon concert she saw with Dad on their first date, and I'll have an overpowering déjà vu. Not just a sense that I've heard the story before, but that I've lived it. I can picture myself sitting on the riverbank as Dad pulls a hot-pink coho out of the water, even though Dad was all of twelve at the time. Or I can hear the feedback when Dead Moon played 'DOA' at the X-Ray, even though I've never heard Dead Moon play live, even though the X-Ray Café shut down before I was born. But sometimes the memories feel so real, so visceral, so personal, that I confuse them with my own.

I never told anyone about these 'memories'. Mom

probably would've said that I was there – as one of the eggs in her ovaries. Dad would've joked that he and Mom had tortured me with their stories one too many times and had inadvertently brainwashed me. And Gran would've told me that maybe I *was* there as an angel before I chose to become Mom and Dad's kid.

But now I wonder. And now I hope. Because when I go, I want to remember Kim. And I want to remember her like this: telling a funny story, fighting with her crazy mom, being cheered on by punkers, rising to the occasion, finding little pockets of strength in herself that she had no idea she possessed.

Adam is a different story. Remembering Adam would be like losing him all over again, and I'm not sure if I can bear that on top of everything else.

Kim's up to the part of Operation Distraction, when Brooke Vega and a dozen assorted punks descended upon the hospital. She tells me that before they got to the ICU, she was so scared of getting into trouble, but how when she burst inside the ward, she'd felt exhilarated. When the guard had grabbed her, she hadn't been scared at all. 'I kept thinking, what's the worst that could happen? I go to jail. Mom has a conniption. I get grounded for a year.' She stops for a minute. 'But after what's happened today, that would be nothing. Even going to jail would be easy compared to losing you.'

I know that Kim's telling me this to try to keep me alive. She probably doesn't realize that in a weird way, her remark frees me, just like Gramps's permission did. I know it will be awful for Kim when I die, but I also think about what she said, about not being scared, about jail being easy compared to losing me. And that's how I know that Kim will be OK. Losing me will hurt; it will be the kind of pain that won't feel real at first, and when it does, it will take her breath away. And the rest of her senior year will probably suck, what with her getting all that cloying your-best-friend's-dead sympathy that will drive her so crazy, and also because really, we are each other's only close friend at school. But she'll deal. She'll move on. She'll leave Oregon. She'll go to college. She'll make new friends. She'll fall in love. She'll become a photographer, the kind who never has to go on a helicopter. And I bet she'll be a stronger person because of what she's lost today. I have a feeling that once you live through something like this, you become a little bit invincible.

I know that makes me a bit of a hypocrite. If that's the case, shouldn't I stay? Soldier through it? Maybe if I'd had some practice, maybe if I'd had more devastation in my life, I would be more prepared to go on. It's not that my life has been perfect. I've had disappointments and I've been lonely and frustrated and angry and all the crappy stuff everyone feels. But in terms of heartbreak, I've been spared. I've never toughened up enough to handle what I'd have to handle if I were to stay.

Kim is now telling me about being rescued from certain incarceration by Willow. As she describes how Willow took charge of the whole hospital, there is such admiration in her voice. I picture Kim and Willow becoming friends, even though there are twenty years between them. It makes me happy to imagine them drinking tea or going to the movies together, still connected to each other by the invisible chain of a family that no longer exists.

Now Kim is listing all the people who are at the hospital or who have been, during the course of the day, ticking them off with her fingers: 'Your grandparents and aunts, uncles, and cousins. Adam and Brooke Vega and the various rabble-rousers who came with her. Adam's bandmates Mike and Fitzy and Liz and her girlfriend, Sarah, all of whom have been downstairs in the waiting room since they got heaved out of the ICU. Professor Christie, who drove down and stayed half the night before driving back so she could sleep a few hours and shower and make some morning appointment she had. Henry and the baby, who are on their way over right now because the baby woke up at five in the morning and Henry called us and said that he could not stay at home any longer. And me and Mom,' Kim concludes. 'Shoot. I lost count of how many people that was. But it was a lot. And more have called and asked to come, but your aunt Diane told them to wait. She says that we're making enough nuisance of ourselves. And I think by "us", she means me and Adam.' Kim stops and smiles for a split second. Then she makes this funny noise, a cross between a cough and a throat-clearing. I've heard her make this sound before; it's what she does when she's summoning her courage, getting ready to jump off the rocks and into the bracing river water.

'I do have a point to all this,' she continues. 'There are like twenty people in that waiting room right now. Some of them are related to you. Some of them are not. But we're all your family.'

She stops now. Leans over me so that the wisps of her hair tickle my face. She kisses me on the forehead. '*You still have a family*,' she whispers.

*

Last summer, we hosted an accidental Labor Day party at our house. It had been a busy season. Camp for me. Then we'd gone to Gran's family's Massachusetts retreat. I felt like I had barely seen Adam and Kim all summer. My parents were lamenting that they hadn't seen Willow and Henry and the baby in months. 'Henry says she's starting to walk,' Dad noted that morning. We were all sitting in the living room in front of the fan, trying not to melt. Oregon was having a record heat wave. It was ten in the morning and pushing ninety degrees.

Mom looked up at the calendar. 'She's ten months old already. Where has the time gone?' Then she looked at Teddy and me. 'How is it humanly possible that I have a daughter who's starting her senior year in high school? How in the hell can my baby boy be starting second grade?'

'I'm not a baby,' Teddy shot back, clearly insulted.

'Sorry, kid, unless we have another one, you'll always be my baby.'

'Another one?' Dad asked with mock alarm.

'Relax. I'm kidding – for the most part,' Mom said. 'Let's see how I feel when Mia leaves for college.'

'I'm gonna be eight in December. Then I'm a man and you'll have to call me "Ted",' Teddy reported.

'Is that so?' I laughed, spraying orange juice through my nose.

'That's what Casey Carson told me,' Teddy said, his mouth set into a determined line.

My parents and I groaned. Casey Carson was Teddy's best friend, and we all liked him a lot and thought his parents seemed like such nice people, so we didn't get how they could give their child such a ridiculous name.

'Well, if Casey Carson says so,' I said, giggling, and soon Mom and Dad were laughing, too.

'What's so funny?' Teddy demanded.

'Nothing, Little Man,' Dad said. 'It's just the heat.'

'Can we still do sprinklers today?' Teddy asked. Dad had promised him he could run through the sprinklers that afternoon even though the governor had asked everyone in the state to conserve water this summer. That request had peeved Dad, who claimed that we Oregonians suffer eight months of rain a year and should be exempt from ever worrying about water conservation.

'Damn straight you can,' Dad said. 'Flood the place if you want.'

Teddy seemed placated. 'If the baby can walk, then she can walk through the sprinklers. Can she come into the sprinklers with me?'

Mom looked at Dad. 'That's not a bad idea,' she said. 'I think Willow's off today.'

'We could have a barbecue,' Dad said. 'It is Labor Day and grilling in this heat would certainly qualify as labor.'

'Plus, we've got a freezer full of steaks from when your father decided to order that side of beef,' Mom said. 'Why not?'

'Can Adam come?' I asked.

'Of course,' Mom said. 'We haven't seen much of your young man lately.'

'I know,' I said. 'Things are starting to happen for the band,' I said. At the time I was excited about it. Genuinely and completely. Gran had only recently planted the seed of Juilliard in my head, but it hadn't taken root. I hadn't decided to apply yet. Things with Adam had not gotten weird yet.

'If the rock star can handle a humble picnic with squares like us,' Dad joked.

'If he can handle a square like me, he can handle squares like you,' I joked back. 'I think I'll invite Kim, too.'

'The more the merrier,' Mom said. 'We'll make it a blowout like in the olden days.'

'When dinosaurs roamed the earth?' Teddy asked.

'Exactly,' Dad said. 'When dinosaurs roamed the earth and your mom and I were young.'

About twenty people showed up. Henry, Willow, the baby, Adam, who brought Fitzy, Kim, who brought a cousin visiting from New Jersey, plus a whole bunch of friends of my parents whom they had not seen in ages. Dad hauled our ancient barbecue out of the basement and spent the afternoon scrubbing it. We grilled up steaks and, this being Oregon, tofu pups and veggie burgers. There was watermelon, which we kept cool in a bucket of ice, and a salad made with vegetables from the organic farm that some of Mom and Dad's friends had started. Mom and I made three pies with wild blackberries that Teddy and I had picked. We drank Pepsi out of these old-fashioned bottles that Dad had found at some ancient country store, and I swear they tasted better than the regular kind. Maybe it was because it was so hot, or that the party was so last minute, or maybe because everything tastes better on the grill, but it was one of those meals that you know you'll remember.

When Dad turned on the sprinkler for Teddy and the baby, everyone else decided to run through it. We left it on so long that the brown grass turned into a big slippery puddle and I wondered if the governor himself might come and tell us off. Adam tackled me and we laughed and squirmed around on the lawn. It was so hot, I didn't bother changing into dry clothes, just kept dousing myself whenever I got too sweaty. By the end of the day, my sundress was stiff. Teddy had taken his shirt off and had streaked himself with mud. Dad said he looked like one of the boys from *Lord of the Flies*.

When it started to get dark, most people left to catch the fireworks display at the university or to see a band called Oswald Five-0 play in town. A handful of people, including Adam, Kim, Willow, and Henry, stayed. When it cooled off, Dad lit a campfire on the lawn, and we roasted marshmallows. Then the musical instruments appeared. Dad's snare drum from the house, Henry's guitar from his car, Adam's spare guitar from my room. Everyone was jamming together, singing songs: Dad's songs, Adam's songs, old Clash songs, old Wipers songs. Teddy was dancing around, the blond of his hair reflecting the golden flames. I remember watching it all and getting that tickling in my chest and thinking to myself: *This is what happiness feels like.*

At one point, Dad and Adam stopped playing and I caught them whispering about something. Then they went inside, to get more beer, they claimed. But when they returned they were carrying my cello.

'Oh, no, I'm not giving a concert,' I said.

'We don't want you to,' Dad said. 'We want you to play with us.'

'No way,' I said. Adam had occasionally tried to get me to 'jam' with him and I always refused. Lately he'd started joking about us playing air-guitar–air-cello duets, which was about as far as I was willing to go.

'Why not, Mia?' Kim said. 'Are you such a classical-music snob?'

'It's not that,' I said, suddenly feeling panicked. 'It's just that the two styles don't fit together.'

'Says who?' Mom asked, her eyebrows raised.

'Yeah, who knew you were such a musical segregationist?' Henry joked.

Willow rolled her eyes at Henry and turned to me. 'Pretty please,' she said as she rocked the baby to sleep in her lap. 'I never get to hear you play anymore.'

'C'mon, Mee,' Henry said. 'You're among family.'

'Totally,' Kim said.

Adam took my hand and caressed the inside of my wrist with his fingers. 'Do it for me. I really want to play with you. Just once.'

I was about to shake my head, to reaffirm that my cello had no place among the jamming guitars, no place in the punk-rock world. But then I looked out at Mom, who was smirking at me, as if issuing a challenge, and Dad, who was tapping on his pipe, pretending to be nonchalant so as not to apply any pressure, and Teddy, who was jumping up and down – though I think it was because he was hopped up on marshmallows, not because he had any desire to hear me play – and Kim and Willow and Henry all peering at me like this really mattered, and Adam, looking as awed and proud as he always did when he listened to me play. And I was a little scared of falling on my face, of not blending, of making bad music. But everyone was looking at me so intently, wanting me to join in so much, and I realized that sounding bad wasn't the worst thing in the world that could happen.

203

So I played. And even though you wouldn't think it, the cello didn't sound half bad with all those guitars. In fact, it sounded pretty amazing.

7:16 a.m.

It's morning. And inside the hospital, there's a different kind of dawn, a rustling of covers, a clearing of the eyes. In some ways, the hospital never goes to sleep. The lights stay on and the nurses stay awake, but even though it's still dark outside, you can tell that things are waking up. The doctors are back, yanking on my eyelids, shining their lights at me, frowning as they scribble notes in my chart as though I've let them down.

I don't care anymore. I'm tired of this all, and it will be over soon. The social worker is back on duty again, too. It looks like the night's sleep had little impact on her. Her eyes are still heavy, her hair a kinky mess. She reads my chart and listens to updates from the nurses on my bumpy night, which seems to make her even more tired. The nurse with the blue-black skin is also back. She greeted me by telling me how glad she was to see me this morning, how she'd been thinking about me last night, hoping I'd be here. Then she noticed the bloodstain on my blanket and *tsked tsked* before hustling off to get me a new one.

After Kim left, there haven't been any more visitors. I guess Willow has run out of people to lobby me with. I wonder if this deciding business is something that all the nurses are aware of. Nurse Ramirez sure knew about it. And I think the nurse with me now knows it, too, judging by how congratulatory she's acting that I made it through the night. And Willow seems like she knows it, too, with the way she's been marching everyone through here. I like these nurses so much. I hope they will not take my decision personally.

I am so tired now that I can barely blink my eyes. It's all just a matter of time, and part of me wonders why I'm delaying the inevitable. But I know why. I'm waiting for Adam to come back. Though it seems like he has been gone for an eternity, it's probably only been an hour. And he asked me to wait, so I will. That's the least I can do for him.

My eyes are closed so I hear him before I see him. I hear the raspy, quick rushes of his lungs. He is panting like he just ran a marathon. Then I smell the sweat on him, a clean musky scent that I'd bottle and wear as perfume if I could. I open my eyes. Adam has closed his. But the lids are puffy and pink, so I know what he's been doing. Is that why he went away? To cry without my seeing?

He doesn't so much sit in the chair as fall into it, like clothes heaped onto the floor at the end of a long day. He covers his face with his hands and takes deep breaths to steady himself. After a minute, he drops his hands into his lap. 'Just listen,' he says with a voice that sounds like shrapnel.

I open my eyes wide now. I sit up as much as I can. And I listen.

'Stay.' With that one word, Adam's voice catches, but he swallows the emotion and pushes forward. 'There's no word for what happened to you. There's no good side of it. But there is something to live for. And I'm not talking about me. It's just . . . I don't know. Maybe I'm talking shit. I know I'm in shock. I know I haven't digested what happened to your parents, to Teddy . . .' When he says *Teddy*, his voice cracks and an avalanche of tears tumbles down his face. And I think: *I love you.*

I hear him take gulpfuls of air to steady himself. And then he continues: 'All I can think about is how fucked up it would be for your life to end here, now. I mean, I know that your life is fucked up no matter what now, for ever. And I'm not dumb enough to think that I can undo that, that anyone can. But I can't wrap my mind around the notion of you not getting old, having kids, going to Juilliard, getting to play that cello in front of a huge audience, so that they can get the chills the way I do every time I see you pick up your bow, every time I see you smile at me.

'If you stay, I'll do whatever you want. I'll quit the band, go with you to New York. But if you need me to go away, I'll do that, too. I was talking to Liz and she said maybe coming back to your old life would just be too painful, that maybe it'd be easier for you to erase us. And that would suck, but I'd do it. I can lose you like that if I don't lose you today. I'll let you go. If you stay.'

Then it is Adam who lets go. His sobs burst like fists pounding against tender flesh.

I close my eyes. I cover my ears. I cannot watch this. I cannot hear this.

But then, it is no longer Adam that I hear. It's that sound, the low moan that in an instant takes flight and turns into something sweet. It's the cello. Adam has placed head-phones over my lifeless ears and is laying an iPod down on my chest. He's apologizing, saying that he knows this isn't my favorite but it was the best he could do. He turns up the volume so I can hear the music floating across the morning air. Then he takes my hand.

It is Yo-Yo Ma. *Andante con poco e moto rubato*. The low piano plays almost as if in warning. In comes the cello, like a heart bleeding. And it's like something inside of me implodes.

I am sitting around the breakfast table with my family, drinking hot coffee, laughing at Teddy's chocolate-chip mustache. The snow is blowing outside.

I am visiting a cemetery. Three graves under a tree on a hill overlooking the river.

I am lying with Adam, my head on his chest, on a sandy bank next to the river.

I am hearing people say the word *orphan* and realize that they're talking about me.

I am walking through New York City with Kim, the skyscrapers casting shadows on our faces.

I am holding Teddy on my lap, tickling him as he giggles so hard he keels over.

I am sitting with my cello, the one Mom and Dad gave me after my first recital. My fingers caress the wood and the pegs, which time and touch have worn smooth. My bow is poised over the strings now. I am looking at my hand, waiting to start playing.

I am looking at my hand, being held by Adam's hand.

Yo-Yo Ma continues to play, and it's like the piano and cello are being poured into my body, the same way that the IV and blood transfusions are. And the memories of my life as it was, and the flashes of it as it might be, are coming so fast and furious. I feel like I can no longer keep up with them but they keep coming and everything is colliding, until I cannot take it anymore. Until I cannot be like this one second longer.

There is a blinding flash, a pain that rips through me for one searing instant, a silent scream from my broken body. For the first time, I can sense how fully agonizing staying will be.

But then I feel Adam's hand. Not sense it, but feel it. I'm not sitting huddled in the chair anymore. I'm lying on my back in the hospital bed, one again with my body.

Adam is crying and somewhere inside of me I am crying, too, because I'm feeling things at last. I'm feeling not just the physical pain, but all that I have lost, and it is profound and catastrophic and will leave a crater in me that nothing will ever fill. But I'm also feeling all that I have in my life, which includes what I have lost, as well as the great unknown of what life might still bring me. And it's all too much. The feelings pile up, threatening to crack my chest wide open. The only way to survive them is to concentrate on Adam's hand. Grasping mine.

And suddenly I just *need* to hold his hand more than I've ever needed anything in this world. Not just be held by it, but hold it back. I aim every remaining ounce of energy into my right hand. I'm weak, and this is so hard. It's the hardest thing I will ever have to do. I summon all the love I have ever felt, I summon all the strength that Gran and Gramps and Kim and the nurses and Willow have given me. I summon all the breath that Mom, Dad, and Teddy would fill me with if they could. I summon all my own strength, focus it like a laser beam into the fingers and palm of my right hand. I picture my hand stroking Teddy's hair, grasping a bow poised above my cello, interlaced with Adam's.

And then I squeeze.

I slump back, spent, unsure of whether I just did what I did. Of what it means. If it registered. If it matters.

But then I feel Adam's grip tighten, so that the grasp of his hand feels like it is holding my entire body. Like it could lift me up right out of this bed. And then I hear the sharp intake of his breath followed by the sound of his voice. It's the first time today I can truly hear him.

'Mia?' he asks.

Acknowledgments

Several people came together in a short amount of time to make *If I Stay* possible. It starts with Gillian Aldrich, who started crying (in a good way) when I told her about my idea. This proved to be quite a good motivator to get started.

Tamara Glenny, Eliza Griswold, Kim Sevcik and Sean Smith took time out of their hectic schedules to read early drafts of my work and to offer much-needed encouragement. For that and for their enduring generosity and friendship, I love and thank them. Some people help you keep your head straight; Marjorie Ingall helps me keep my heart straight, and for that I love and thank her. Thank you also to Jana and Moshe Banin.

Sarah Burnes is my agent in the truest sense of the word, harnessing her formidable intelligence, insight, passion and warmth to shepherd the words that I write to the people who should read them. She, along with the superb Courtney

Hammer and Stephanie Cabot, has made miracles happen where this book is concerned. Across the pond, Caspian Dennis and Abner Stein worked miracles of their own.

Selina Walker at Transworld was the first publisher to believe in this book and for that I am indebted to her as well as to the wonderful Clare Argar and Annie Eaton at Random House Children's Books. Back in the US at Penguin, my thanks go to my extraordinary editor, Julie Strauss-Gabel, as well as Don Weisberg and the indefatigable sales, marketing, publicity and design teams who worked so hard for this book.

Music is a huge part of this story, and I drew a lot of inspiration from Yo-Yo Ma – whose own work informs much of Mia's story – and from Glen Hansard and Marketa Irglova, whose song 'Falling Slowly' I probably listened to more than 200 times while working on the book.

Thanks to my Oregon contingent: Greg and Diane Rios, who have been our compatriots through all this. John and Peg Christie, whose grace, dignity, and generosity continue to move me. Jennifer Larson, MD, an old friend and, as luck would have it, an emergency-room doctor, who enlightened me about Glasgow Coma Scales, among other medical details.

Thanks to my parents – Lee and Ruth Forman – and my siblings – Tamar Schamhart and Greg Forman – all of whom are my cheerleaders and most steadfast fans, who ignore my failings (professional ones, anyhow) and celebrate my successes as if they were their own (which they are).

I didn't immediately recognize how much of this book is about the way parents transform their lives for their children. Willa Tucker teaches me this lesson every day and is occasionally forgiving when I am too absorbed playing make believe in my head to play make believe with her.

Without my husband, Nick Tucker, none of this would be. I owe him everything.

Finally, my deepest thanks go to R.D.T.J., who inspire me in so many ways and who show me every single day that there is such a thing as immortality.

The Story Behind The Story

Once upon a time there was a family: a mother, a father, a boy like Teddy and a baby. And once upon a time there was a snowy day. And a drive in a car. And a devastating car accident. And an unfathomable tragedy.

Once upon a time one of those family members held on a little longer, though by the time the news reached me, all the way across the country in New York City, the tragedy was complete. But the child's act of tenacity, followed by his surrender, haunted me. Did he know what had happened to the rest of his family? Did he choose to go with them?

Once upon a time there was a vibrant family of four. And then there wasn't. And what was left was heartbreak. Mine, and other people's.

But what was left was also important, in that it became something with which I simply could not come to terms from outside my own grief. As friends from around the country spontaneously gathered in the Oregon town where our friends had once lived, as we rushed headlong into the hell of our loss, I found a clarity, a guidance, a moral compass.

How would the tragedy change us? How would *we* change us? How would we rise to the occasion – not just of their deaths but of our lives? And, as I experienced a depth of grief unknown to me previously, I found something that felt divine. Was this our newly departed friends watching out for us? Was this God?

Of course, this transcendent grieving doesn't last. Gloom descends, the awfulness of your loss hits you, again and again. Real life gets on with itself. And eventually your loss normalizes, it integrates into part of your everyday life, and you find yourself three or five years later doing OK, changed but . . . but still able to hear your friends' voices, still telling stories about them, still thinking of them every day. And still pondering questions about them – like, did one of them choose to die knowing the rest of his family had been obliterated?

It was out of the fog of this persistent question that one day, almost seven years later, a stranger popped into my consciousness.

Her name was Mia. She was seventeen years old. And a cello player (news to me; I knew nothing about the cello and not so much about classical music). And she had no relation whatsoever to the people I knew. But the minute I met her I knew she was going to take me on a journey, to answer that question that had been living in me for years: *What would I do if I had to choose?* I didn't know what Mia's answer would be when I started the book, though I knew it would be her own decision based upon the life that she and I were creating together.

People often ask me if the book was emotional or difficult to write. Emotional, yes. I typed through a lot of tears. But it was the opposite of difficult. Some of that grace from the days after the tragedy returned. Maybe that was because I was creating characters somewhat based on friends I loved and so I was deeply ensconced in their world again. It was as if they were right there in the room with me as I wrote.

And in a way they were. In a way, they have never left me. And that's just it, isn't it? That's how we manage to survive loss. Because love never dies; it never goes away; and it never fades. As long as you hang onto it.

Gayle Forman
January 2010

Behind the Music

Music is a major part of *If I Stay*, with both rock and classical references and allusions woven throughout the story. If you want to hear more of the songs mentioned in the book, head to www.gayleforman.com. But if you want to learn *why* I chose to include certain songs or mentioned specific artists or just get some music recommendations, here's a behind-the-scenes listening tour.

Page 8: 'School's Out' by Alice Cooper: When he hears that school's closed for the day, Teddy sings the requisite song for ditching school. I still can't imagine him joyfully bellowing this out without getting a pit in my stomach.

Page 10: Jonathan Richman: In the car, Dad suggests – and Teddy rejects – playing Jonathan Richman, whom Mia describes as her parents' 'musical patron saint'. OK, he's actually mine! Rockin', sweet, tender, edgy, goofy, Jonathan is considered by many to be the Godfather of Punk. Go listen to his debut, *Jonathan Richman and the Modern Lovers*;

released in 1976, it *still* sounds fresh. Tunes like 'I'm a Little Dinosaur' also make him a fave among children.

Page 10: Teddy begs to listen to SpongeBob, by which I was actually referring to the very cool Flaming Lips song 'SpongeBob and Patrick Confront the Psychic Wall of Energy' from the *SpongeBob* Soundtrack. Teddy has impeccable taste in music, too.

Page 11: Beethoven's Cello Sonata no. 3: This is the piece that comes on right before the accident, the one that Mia was meant to be practicing that day. I chose it because it announces that Mia is a serious and accomplished cellist.

Page 20: Tchaikovsky's 'Dance of the Sugar Plum Fairy'. This is what Mia plays at her first recital when she's eight. It seemed like one of those popular pieces kids would choose to play – and mangle. Not Mia, though.

Page 32: The Icelandic art band Adam plays for Mia is Sigur Rós.

Page 32: Yo-Yo Ma, 'Le Grand Tango'. Recently, the master of all things cello has been doing all kinds of cool experimental crossover stuff, so I decided that he'd be playing some of his more contemporary work – which seemed like something that would move Adam at the concert he and Mia go to on their first date. But the tango recordings were done in 1997, so strictly speaking Yo-Yo Ma would not have been playing them in 2005. I'm afraid I cheated a little here.

Page 35: To me (and the doctors), Mia's surgery seemed like a battle, hence Wagner's 'Ride of the Valkyries'.

Page 43: Mia's Juilliard audition pieces are all taken straight from the school's website, which lists a menu of what applicants can play for their auditions. I chose the Ennio Morricone piece from *The Mission* because when I saw that movie when I was sixteen, I loved the score so much, I immediately ran out and bought a cassette of the soundtrack.

Pages 104–105: Although Mia namedrops classical musicians like Dvořák and Schubert, I have to admit that personally I'm much more comfortable firing off a bunch of rock divas like Mia's mother does when Mia asks her who the hottest rocker girl she can think of is – and she replies with a list that includes Kathleen Hanna (of Bikini Kill and Le Tigre), Joan Jett (Kristen Stewart is playing her in a movie about the all-girl rock band *The Runaways*) and Lucinda Williams.

Page 114: 'Something in the Way' by Nirvana. When Kim wanted to play Mia a modern band that used a cellist, there was no question who to pick. Nirvana from the *MTV Unplugged in New York* album.

Page 125: 'Girlfriend in a Coma' by The Smiths. Because a little gallows humor never hurts.

Page 127: 'Eraser' by Bikini. This is a fake song by a fake band. There is no Bikini. And there is no Shooting Star, either. I took the name Shooting Star from a short-lived band my husband played in called the Redmond Shooting Stars. When I checked to see if there was an actual band called Shooting Star, I was surprised to see there was only some defunct Euro hair band from the eighties.

Page 137: Melvins; Earth. I must come clean now. I *really* dislike the heavy, heavy sound of these two bands. But it seemed like Mia's mother would totally want to labor to them.

Page 150: 'Wind Beneath My Wings' by Bette Midler. Just hearing that synthesizer at the beginning of this song activates my gag reflex. Just hearing the opening notes of 'Amazing Grace', though, never fails to raise the hairs on the back of my neck - in a good way.

Page 151: 'Three Little Birds' by Bob Marley. I never really thought of this as a funereal song until I thought of Kerry, and then it just fit. Characters, even minor ones, speak to you.

Page 152: Henry requests the Mr T Experience at his funeral. Specifically I was thinking of the song 'Love American Style'. Someone I was in love with made me a mixed tape with that track on it and to this day some of the lyrics are like the pinnacle of romance to me. I can see Henry making a mixed tape for Willow so that's why I had him request this band.

Page 153: 'P.S. You Rock My World' by The Eels. Willow's personal funeral selection is off one of my favorite albums, *Electro-Shock Blues*, a record about grieving that helped me through a hard time in my own life.

Page 153: Mozart's Requiem. Mia's funeral choice. Haunting. Intense. Beautiful. Just like my girl.

Page 153: 'Fire and Rain' by James Taylor. Classic folky tear-jerker song. Would be cheesy if it weren't so good.

Page 168–169: 'Waiting for Vengeance'. Even though Dad's band is nameless, and fictional, this particular lyric is adapted from an actual song by Oswald-Five-0. I suck at writing lyrics and this particular song worked eerily well for the story. You can go to my website and download this song for free.

Page 193: 'D.O.A.' by Dead Moon. This is the song that Mia swears she can 'remember' her parents listening to on their first date (before she was born). Dead Moon is this great, semi-obscure garage band from Portland, and while I recognize that including a track titled 'D.O.A.' might be metaphoric overkill, it's my favorite Dead Moon song so I did it anyway.

Page 202: Clash. Many of you will know The Clash, and if you don't, go listen to *London Calling* now. The Wipers are a less-known punk band from Portland, whom rockers like Mia's dad and Adam would worship. Pick up a copy of *Is This Real?* if you want to rock it old-school northwest style.

Page 207: *Andante con moto e poco rubato* by George Gershwin, performed by Yo-Yo Ma. Finding the piece that would bring Mia back was a challenge. First, I had to figure which Yo-Yo Ma album Adam would be able to readily download in the middle of the night. I decided that Adam would choose compilations. So I downloaded a couple of likely comps and then I lay down on my couch, closed my eyes, and listened. The song that gave me the strongest emotional reaction – goose bumps, palpitations – won.

A Conversation with Chloë Grace Moretz

When *If I Stay* film rights were first optioned, screenwriter Shauna Cross and I were musing about the young actresses who might play Mia. "Too bad Chloë Moretz is so young because she's incredible," Shauna said. At the time, Moretz had just wowed the world with her performance as Hit Girl in *Kick-Ass*, but she was only thirteen.

Sometimes films take a while to make their way into production, and in this case, those few years worked in our favor because while Mia stayed the same age, Chloë got older, and became the perfect age to play Mia.

Watching her work, I was blown away. So much of the acting took place in the silences, in the beats between lines, in her expressions. It was very clear she'd inhabited the character on a cellular level. And when I sat down to talk to her a few months after the film wrapped, I was once again blown away by how much thought this young woman put into every aspect of the role.

Beware: spoilers below.

Gayle Forman: You've said that you really connected to Mia when you first read the book and script for *If I Stay*. Why was that?

Chloë Grace Moretz: Mia reminds of the girl I am--behind the acting, behind the this and the that, she's me--this girl who is passionate and young and who wants to live life but is very driven. She knows exactly what she wants and how she's going to get it. Mia was five or six when she first touched the cello and I was five when I started acting. I always felt very close to her in that sense.

GF: When I got to know you a little bit, I did see this dichotomy: movie star Chloë and regular Chloë. I know it seems like a cliché, but you seem like a normal girl who is also very driven and smart about what she wants to do. That's such an interesting parallel between you and Mia.

CGM: It definitely made it easy for me to jump into Mia's mind.

GF: Very early on, you sent me a message in which you wrote: I can't wait to actively start learning the cello. It's such an integral part of Mia's being, and a must in order to portray her. You did study cello. How did that connect you to the character?

CGM: The cello really was an integral part of who Mia is. It's her conscience, almost. When she plays it, everything that she wants to say and can't, everything she is feeling deep inside and can't let out, becomes apparent. When she's mad at her parents, she plays better than ever. When she's in the deepest part of her relationship with Adam, she plays better than she has in ages. It's like how acting is for me in that sense. That's why I wanted to really embody a cellist. It's such a personal instrument for so many classical cellists who I've met. They almost breathe with the cello. When the bow stroke goes down, they breathe out; when it goes up, they breathe in. It's this beautiful fluid thing they don't realize is happening until someone else mentions it to them.

GF: That makes sense. The cello is such an emotional instrument. When you listen to it, it seems to translate the feelings of the person playing or composing. That breathing into it, it's almost as if you're pouring yourself into it as you play.

CGM: I think it's one of the deepest and most emotional and realistic instruments. The violin can be so sweet. It doesn't have that depth. The viola ventures into that depth, but it still has that pitch. What's so interesting about the cello is that if it's played in the right way, it can be a violin. It can also be a bass. When it's played a certain way, it can sound like a guitar. It is so many instruments packed into one.

GF: I became a classical music fan after Mia arrived in my head, fully formed, a cellist. But you, you've always been into classical, right?

CGM: Oh, totally. I've been a fan since I was a little kid. I always listen to classical music. I always wanted to learn to play an instrument, but I've never had the time. To be able to do it during a movie . . . . I found it so much fun to learn—or start to learn—a classical instrument.

GF: The film, like the book, is divided into two parts: the present, which follows Mia after the accident, when she is mostly outside of her body; and the flashback scenes, showing Mia as a musician, a friend, a daughter, a sister, and of course, a girlfriend, as she falls in love with Adam. Did it feel like playing two completely different roles?

CGM: Totally. The Mia you meet in the flashbacks is a girl. She's just experiencing love for the first time. She's just experiencing success in the classical world. She's becoming a woman. The Mia you see in the hospital, she's a shell of who Mia used to be. She's not a person, per se. She's like a thought, this resolved, angelic person.

GF: Which was more challenging, present tense ghost Mia or past tense Mia, who had to make herself very vulnerable, especially falling in love with Adam?

CGM: Because Jamie [Blackley] is such a nice guy, it was easy to do all that. It was so simple. Mireille [Enos] is an amazing person. It was easy for her to play my mom. Josh [Leonard] was so great and Jakob [Davies] was the best little kid. That stuff came really naturally. What was definitely more difficult was embodying the sense of losing them all. That level of loneliness is very deep and very real. It's just pure devastation. I think it's really interesting to have to portray that. And it's hard—really, really hard—to do it honestly.

GF: I was there for only that first day of filming the hospital scenes and that was enough for me. It seemed very intense.

CGM: They were long nights in that insane asylum. [The hospital scenes were shot in an old mental hospital.] We shot those scenes at the end of the shoot, so I knew all those people very well. It hit me hard. They're all dead, in a sense. All of that together was just heavy.

GF: There was a scene I added in revision: Mia at the accident scene when she pinches herself and yells "wake up!" I think I sobbed harder writing that scene because by then I knew her and the rest of the characters so well.

CGM: I can imagine that. Even though she's fictionalized, it's so hard.

GF: As an author, you come to love characters. I'm sure it's the same as an actor. Like you said, it was hard that Jakob, Mireille, and Josh were gone, but they're not. They're still around.

CGM: (Laughs) They're still here. No worries.

GF: You've had love interests, but is this the first part you've done where the love story takes center stage?

CGM: One hundred percent. This is my first romantic movie. Which is so fun.

GF: You've mentioned that you felt a responsibility for getting the romance just right.

CGM: I know many people who are invested in this book. A lot of my friends are. I wanted to do it justice. I wanted to make sure Mia came across as honest, not only to a real person, but honest to you and the readers. That's who we're really making the movie for.

GF: How was it? Falling in love with Adam?

CGM: When I was in the hospital, that was serious, but when we were doing all the alive stuff, that was just so fun. We had the best time. Jamie's such a nice guy. It's easy when people are nice and normal. It's easy to just be.

GF: It was amazing to see you do your craft. You'd be goofing around, then all of a sudden, boom, we're shooting and it's game time and you're all in. How do you do that?

CGM: You just do it. When a script is well written, it's easier. And when I know the character really well, it's easier. With Mia, I knew her so well, it was easy for me to pop in and out of her. At the same time, because it was so dark, I badly wanted to goof around for a second, to jump in the wheelchair, or scoot around set and do the stupidest stuff. When an actor is dealing with such dark things, you have to do that; otherwise you'll go a little crazy.

GF: That makes sense.

CGM: It was great to have Liana [Liberato, who plays Kim], who's one of my close friends now, or Jamie to have fun with. Or Paul Berry, the first assistant director. Or R.J. [Cutler], the director, or Alison [Greenspan], the producer. There were so many awesome people on that set. It was a safe, cool environment.

GF: Let's talk a little about R.J. You knew him before he came on board to direct If I Stay, which you'd already been attached to for quite some time.

CGM: I'd been wanting to work with him for a while. I think he's such a brilliant director. And I'd been on this project for a long time. So for it to actually come together with him as director on this perfect project . . . it couldn't have been better. This is not like your typical YA movie. Neither is the book. You needed a guy who was smart and knew classical music and rock music and the emotions and feelings of young people. You can't have this complete stooge who doesn't understand kids, because he is going to write in this older adult mentality. For some reason, R.J. understood so much of what it means to be a teenager. I think it really reads in the movie.

GF: When you bond with the cast and crew, does it spill over into your performance or is it more that it gives you breathing space?

CGM: First of all, it makes you feel more comfortable. And second, it does spill over, because you enjoy them. It's easy. You can just be. You don't have to think, *Oh my god, I* *really don't like this person, but I've got to be their girlfriend or best friend or daughter in this scene.* It's so annoying when you have to do that. When you actually love the people around you—as people, as friends—you don't have to think. You can just do it.

GF: Which scene was the most emotional?

CGM: Finding out that Teddy was dead. That was just so hard. I loved Jakob, and it was heavy for me to think of that. It was very dark. I run down the hall and I collapse on my knees and I'm screaming. Mia is giving up in that moment. Not only is she finding out that Teddy's dead, she's also saying: *To hell with this. I'm done.*

GF: Which scene was the most fun?

CGM: For some reason, I really loved the scene with me and Liana in the coffee shop, talking. It's a quick scene, but we had so much fun that day. It was genuinely one of the most fun days. I don't know why. It was just so much fun.

GF: That's the scene where you tell Kim you have a

boyfriend?

CGM: Yeah. And she's like, "Oh, I already knew."

GF: Now I have a very important question for you. I want you to give it some deep thought before you answer. You had some really cute clothes in the film. Monique Prudhomme [the costume designer] gave Mia a really great wardrobe. Can you pick a favorite outfit?

CGM: This is easy for me. It's the first time I go to see Adam's band play. I'm wearing a tight striped shirt, a little belt with a little skirt, tights and boots, and I have a little blazer that I take off in the middle of it. I love that outfit.

GF: I loved all Mia's outfits. All the little blazers. A little preppy, a little grungy. So cute.

CGM: Not over-the-top preppy, but not a cool kid. Just Mia.

A Conversation with Jamie Blackley

As soon as it was announced that *If I Stay* was being made into a movie, fans started asking me whom I pictured as Adam. I never had an answer. I had such a clear idea of Adam in my head and no actor really matched that.

When they started casting, I understood just what a challenge filling this role was. The actor who was to play Adam had to be young. He had to have that combination of charismatic swagger (someone you'd buy as an up-and-coming rock star) and vulnerability. He had to be able to sing and play guitar. (The filmmakers were always adamant that the musicians in the movie could actually play.) He'd have to be able to pull off some heavy-duty acting. And, of course, he had to be hot.

The search for Adam was an international hunt that ultimately led to English actor Jamie Blackley. When I saw his audition scene, it was as if someone had gone into my brain and extracted Adam. And watching him on set, whether in the sweet romantic kissing scenes or the edgier concert scenes, the feeling only grew.

I caught up with Jamie when he was in New York City a few months after the shoot. And I'm going to sound like a cliché again, but just as much as Chloë struck me as a normal (if absurdly talented) girl, Jamie is incredibly talented, totally hot, and also a sweetheart. Kinda like Adam.

Gayle Forman: I recently talked to Chloë about what drew her to Mia, so now I want to know what spark attracted you to Adam?

Jamie Blackley: A lot of stuff that I've done has been about a guy who likes someone, or is in a quick, lustful relationship, as in *And While We Were Here*, which covered just a short space of time. *If I Stay* was more about a personal relationship, which was really interesting. Adam and Mia are together for a year and a half, two years. You know a person by that time, and to be able to convey that in a truthful way is quite challenging.

GF: So it was the love story?

JB: It was the love story.

GF: What about the music element? Was that a draw? Was it intimidating?

JB: I'd done quite a bit of stuff involving music before, characters who played music, so it wasn't really intimidating. It was exciting to know that I'd be playing concerts, because I hadn't really done that before. And also as the movie progressed, the band I was in would progress as well. It really felt like that because we had all these rehearsals, and the shows got bigger, and by the end, the band could play the music live. Which we enjoyed.

GF: You already played guitar and sang, but you still had to do a fair amount of training, right?

JB: I would be sent the songs and the chord sheets to learn them. Then I'd have lessons with a guy named Simon Tong, who's played with Gorillaz and Blur. I'd go to his house and we'd spend a couple of hours and he'd teach me the songs and get me comfortable with them so I would be relaxed when I was playing them. That was a really cool experience, to learn from someone who's been in it for so long. It was really special. I'm not an amazing guitarist. I can just get by.

GF: I don't know about that. I heard your guitar playing really came along. And you really rocked it in the concert scenes.

JB: It did come along. I had a guitar in my hotel room. If you're a guitarist, you get home and you see the guitar there and you're watching TV and you just play along. I think that practice element made me a bit better. I got used to playing every day.

GF: Was there band practice before you started filming?

JB: I recorded all of the songs [from Adam's band] in the studio before we shot the movie. Then, before we shot a gig scene, we would have a band rehearsal. We'd all get together and go into the rehearsal room for three or four hours, and we'd practice the song we were going to shoot. It was genuine band practice.

GF: The guitar, band practice, did that help you discover the character of Adam?

JB: By the time we got to shooting, I was used to being in a studio and singing and playing guitar every day, and that's what Adam would do. He'd spend every day playing the guitar, thinking about music, listening to music. That's what I did. And I'd go to see shows. I saw more gigs in Vancouver than I have in the past two years. Being around musicians as well, it rubs off on you.

GF: Speaking of musicians, you seemed to have a good time with your band mates. You even had a bromance.

JB: Yes, I did have a bromance with Mr. Ben Klassen. He's such a special guy. They're all such special people. It was great to be around people who hadn't done something like this before because I think the excitement rubs off on you. It was their first experience on a film set; that excitement just makes you feel excited. It's just a refreshing experience.

GF: Readers might not know that none of your band mates were professional actors. They're all musicians. Not one had ever been in a film before.

JB: How great is that? Ben works construction with his dad, and Ali (Milner) plays a bunch of gigs in hotels around Vancouver. Ryan (Stephenson) and Tom (Vanderkam) make music, and Ryan teaches. And then all of a sudden they're in the middle of a movie set.

GF: This shoot seemed to be a first, or a different experience, for a lot of people. A different kind of role for you, Mireille, and Joshua. Chloë, too. It was my first adaptation. And it was the feature debut of our director, R.J. Cutler, who put his blood and guts into it.

JB: He cared so much about it. I got that as soon as I met him when I was testing. I could see that in him, that he cared so much about it, and that meant that he would care about all of the characters in it. I felt he believed in me and that was so important. Sometimes you're left in the dark a little bit. But he never did that. He always made me feel confident and kept the story relevant, and he let me know where we were coming from and where we were going. Everyone on set was there for the right reasons. Because they believed in what we were doing. It comes out in the end in the work.

GF: I think that's right. And Chloë said that the on-set bonding really alters the shooting experience. Was that true for you?

JB: Yeah. At the end of the day, me and Chloë had to play people in love. How horrible would that have been to do with someone I hated? She's so lovely and she's such a talented girl, and I felt honored, really, to be able to work with her. She was awesome. The fact that we did get on and she was so nice, it made every day at work so easy.

GF: The film is split into two sections: the flashbacks, which are lighter, though you and Mia have some intense scenes together, and the present tense in the hospital, when Adam has some of his most emotional scenes. Did you prefer one over the other?

JB: I don't think I did. We shot all the stuff in the [Hall] house first, and I thought that was a really smart move. We understood what Mia was losing, the battle she had with herself when she's ghost Mia. I got a feel for what this kind of family would be like and what a loving and nice relationship she had with them. And for that all to go, and then we shoot the rest of it. The hospital stuff was difficult. Just being in a hospital is hard. And having her lying there.

GF: The day when you see Mia comatose, what was that like?

JB: People talk about actors trying to get into a certain mode, but when it's all there in front of you—I've got a girl there lying in bed, she's completely unresponsive—it makes it all feel real.

GF: Was there a scene that was the most emotional or challenging?

JB: When I speak to her in the hospital. I don't know how long we shot that for, but it felt like forever. It was so exhausting.

GF: That's the scene where you plead with Mia to stay, and then you completely lose it. How did you summon that level of emotional intensity, over and over?

JB: I wrote a letter. I won't say who it was to. But I'd read it in between takes and that would help me out. And I'd listen to a song that reminded me of something close to my heart.

GF: What song?

JB: "Me," by The 1975. It just does something to me. I saw them in Vancouver when I was there, and then I saw them in London after and they played it live. At that point, it had become such a huge song to me.

GF: While writing *If I Stay*, I'd listen to "Falling Slowly" by Glen Hansard and Markéta Irglová. It would make me cry. And then I'd be ready to write. I'm not sure why it made me so emotional. It's not a sad song, so much as melancholy. But it worked.

JB: Same with mine. The lyrical content of "Me" wasn't relevant in the slightest, but the song just did something.

GF: I love how music is an emotional trigger. After I wrote the book, people asked me if I was a musician. I'm not, never have been, but music has always had an intense emotional impact on me.

JB: It's such a cool medium to evoke any kind of emotion. I wish I could write music. I really can't. I'm not very good at it. I envy anyone who can.

GF: So that was the most difficult scene. Which scene was the most fun to shoot?

JB: That has to be the band's last gig scene. It was so much and there were so many people in the crowd, and I felt like I was in a band at a gig and it was exhilarating. And I think Crystal Palace [the London football team Jamie is obsessed with] won that day. So that was an amazing day. That was so, so much fun.

GF: I was there when you shot that scene. It was electric. I think fans are going to be so excited to see and hear the music leap off the page and they're going to love all the original songs Adam and his band play. They're so catchy and great, and I totally believe this band would be playing them. Did you have a favorite song?

JB: It has to be the last song we play, "Mind." There's a bit in it, like a musical break, where all of us in the band went crazy.

GF: Finally, I have to ask about the sequel, *Where She Went*. While we were filming, I know that you purposely didn't read it, even though it is told from Adam's point of view.

JB: I didn't read it before we shot because I didn't want it to cloud the Adam I play in *If I Stay*. My mum read it, though. She loves it. Says it's her favorite of the two.

GF: And now?

JB: I haven't read it yet. I don't want to get my hopes up!

It well may be that in a difficult hour,
Pinned down by pain and moaning for release,
Or nagged by want past resolution's power,
I might be driven to sell your love for peace,
Or trade the memory of this night for food.
It well may be. I do not think I would.

Excerpt from "Love is not all:
it is not meat nor drink."
BY EDNA ST. VINCENT MILLAY

Every morning I wake up and I tell myself this: *It's just one day, one twenty-four-hour period to get yourself through.* I don't know when exactly I started giving myself this daily pep talk—or why. It sounds like a twelve-step mantra and I'm not in Anything Anonymous, though to read some of the crap they write about me, you'd think I should be. I have the kind of life a lot of people would probably sell a kidney to just experience a bit of. But still, I find the need to remind myself of the temporariness of a day, to reassure myself that I got through yesterday, I'll get through today.

This morning, after my daily prodding, I glance at the minimalist digital clock on the hotel nightstand. It reads 11:47, positively crack-of-dawn for me. But the front desk has already rang with two wake-up calls, followed by a polite-but-firm buzz from our manager, Aldous. Today might be just one day, but it's packed.

I'm due at the studio to lay down a few final guitar tracks for some Internet-only version of the first single of our just-released album. Such a gimmick. Same song, new guitar track, some vocal effects, pay an extra buck for it. "These days, you've gotta milk a dollar out of every dime," the suits at the label are so fond of reminding us.

After the studio, I have a lunch interview with some reporter from *Shuffle*. Those two events are kinda like the bookends of what my life has become: making the music, which I like, and talking about making the music, which I loathe. But they're flip sides of the same coin. When Aldous calls a second time I finally kick off the duvet and grab the prescription bottle from the side table. It's some anti-anxiety thing I'm supposed to take when I'm feeling jittery.

Jittery is how I normally feel. Jittery I've gotten used to. But ever since we kicked off our tour with three shows at Madison Square Garden, I've been feeling something else. Like I'm about to be sucked into something powerful and painful. Vortexy.

Is that even a word? I ask myself.

You're talking to yourself, so who the hell cares? I reply, popping a couple of pills. I pull on some boxers, and go to the door of my room, where a pot of coffee is already waiting. It's been left there by a hotel employee, undoubtedly under strict instructions to stay out of my way.

I finish my coffee, get dressed, and make my way down the service elevator and out the side entrance— the guest-relations manager has kindly provided me with special access keys so I can avoid the scenester parade in the lobby. Out on the sidewalk, I'm greeted by a blast of steaming New York air. It's kind of oppressive, but I like that the air is wet. It reminds me of Oregon, where the rain falls endlessly, and even on the hottest of summer days, blooming white cumulus clouds float above, their shadows reminding you that summer's heat is fleeting, and the rain's never far off.

In Los Angeles, where I live now, it hardly ever rains. And the heat, it's never-ending. But it's a dry heat. People there use this aridness as a blanket excuse for all of the hot, smoggy city's excesses. "It may be a hundred and seven degrees today," they'll brag, "but at least it's a dry heat."

But New York is a wet heat; by the time I reach the studio ten blocks away on a desolate stretch in the West

Fifties, my hair, which I keep hidden under a cap, is damp. I pull a cigarette from my pocket and my hand shakes as I light up. I've had a slight tremor for the last year or so. After extensive medical checks, the doctors declared it nothing more than nerves and advised me to try yoga.

When I get to the studio, Aldous is waiting outside under the awning. He looks at me, at my cigarette, back at my face. I can tell by the way that he's eyeballing me, he's trying to decide whether he needs to be Good Cop or Bad Cop. I must look like shit because he opts for Good Cop.

"Good morning, Sunshine," he says jovially.

"Yeah? What's ever good about morning?" I try to make it sound like a joke.

"Technically, it's afternoon now. We're running late."

I stub out my cigarette. Aldous puts a giant paw on my shoulder, incongruously gentle. "We just want one guitar track on 'Sugar,' just to give it that little something extra so fans buy it all over again." He laughs, shakes his head at what the business has become. "Then you have lunch with *Shuffle,* and we have a photo shoot for that Fashion Rocks thing for the *Times* with the rest of the band around five, and then a quick drinks thing with some money guys at the label, and then I'm off to the airport. Tomorrow, you have a quick little meeting with publicity and merchandising. Just smile and don't say a lot. After that you're on your lonesome until London."

On my lonesome? As opposed to being in the warm bosom of family when we're all together? I say. Only I say it to myself. More and more lately it seems as though the majority of my conversations are with myself. Given half the stuff I think, that's probably a good thing.

But this time I really will be by myself. Aldous and the rest of the band are flying to England tonight. I was supposed to be on the same flight as them until I realized that today was Friday the thirteenth, and I was like no fucking way! I'm dreading this tour enough as is, so I'm not jinxing it further by leaving on the official day of bad luck. So I'd had Aldous book me a day later. We're shooting a video in London and then doing a bunch of press before we start the European leg of our tour, so it's not like I'm missing a show, just a preliminary meeting with our video director. I don't need to hear about his artistic vision. When we start shooting, I'll do what he tells me.

I follow Aldous into the studio and enter a sound-proof booth where it's just me and a row of guitars. On the other side of the glass sit our producer, Stim, and the sound engineers. Aldous joins them. "Okay, Adam," says Stim, "one more track on the bridge and the chorus. Just to make that hook that much more sticky. We'll play with the vocals in the mixing."

"Hooky. Sticky. Got it." I put on my headphones and pick up my guitar to tune up and warm up. I try not to notice that in spite of what Aldous said a few minutes ago, it feels like I'm *already* all on my lonesome. Me alone in a soundproof booth. *Don't overthink it*, I tell myself. *This is how you record in a technologically advanced studio.* The only problem is, I felt the same way a few nights ago at the Garden. Up onstage, in front of eighteen thousand fans, alongside the people who, once upon a time, were part of my family, I felt as alone as I do in this booth.

Still, it could be worse. I start to play and my fingers nimble up and I get off the stool and bang and crank against my guitar, pummel it until it screeches and screams just the way I want it to. Or almost the way I want it to. There's probably a hundred grand's worth of guitars in this room, but none of them sound as good as my old Les Paul Junior—the guitar I'd had for ages, the one I'd recorded our first albums on, the one that, in a fit of stupidity or hubris or whatever, I'd allowed to be auctioned off for charity. The shiny, expensive replacements have never sounded or felt quite right. Still, when I crank it up loud, I do manage to lose myself for a second or two.

But it's over all too soon, and then Stim and the engineers are shaking my hand and wishing me luck on tour, and Aldous is shepherding me out the door and into a town car and we're whizzing down Ninth Avenue to SoHo, to a hotel whose restaurant the publicists from our record label have decided is a good spot for our interview. What, do they think I'm less likely to rant or say something alienating if I'm in an expensive public place? I remember back in the very early days, when the interviewers wrote 'zines or blogs and were fans and mostly wanted to rock-talk—to discuss the *music*—and they wanted to speak to all of us together. More often than not, it just turned into a normal conversation with everyone shouting their opinions over one another. Back then I never worried about guarding my words. But now the reporters interrogate me and the band separately, as though they're cops and they have me and my accomplices in adjacent cells and are trying to get us to implicate one another.

I need a cigarette before we go in, so Aldous and I stand outside the hotel in the blinding midday sun as a crowd of people gathers and checks me out while pretending not to. That's the difference between New York and the rest of the world. People are just as celebrity-crazed as anywhere, but New Yorkers—or at least the ones who consider themselves sophisticates and loiter along the kind of SoHo block I'm standing on now—put on this pretense that they don't care, even as they stare out from their three-hundred-dollar shades. Then they act all disdainful when out-of-towners break the code by rushing up and asking for an autograph as a pair of girls in U Michigan sweatshirts have just done, much to the annoyance of the nearby trio of snobs, who watch the girls and roll their eyes and give me a look of sympathy. As if the *girls* are the problem.

"We need to get you a better disguise, Wilde Man," Aldous says, after the girls, giggling with excitement, flutter away. He's the only one who's allowed to call me that anymore. Before it used to be a general nickname, a takeoff on my last name, Wilde. But once I sort of trashed a hotel room and after that "Wilde Man" became an unshakable tabloid moniker.

Then, as if on cue, a photographer shows up. You can't stand in front of a high-end hotel for more than three minutes before that happens. "Adam! Bryn inside?" A photo of me and Bryn is worth about quadruple one of me alone. But after the first flash goes off, Aldous shoves one hand in front of the guy's lens, and another in front of my face.

As he ushers me inside, he preps me. "The reporter is named Vanessa LeGrande. She's not one of those grizzled types you hate. She's young. Not younger than you, but early twenties, I think. Used to write for a blog before she got tapped by *Shuffle*."

"Which blog?" I interrupt. Aldous rarely gives me detailed rundowns on reporters unless there's a reason.

"Not sure. Maybe Gabber."

"Oh, Al, that's a piece-of-crap gossip site."

"*Shuffle* isn't a gossip site. And this is the cover exclusive."

"Fine. Whatever," I say, pushing through the restaurant doors. Inside it's all low steel-and-glass tables and leather banquettes, like a million other places I've been to. These restaurants think so highly of themselves, but really they're just overpriced, overstylized versions of McDonald's.

"There she is, corner table, the blonde with the streaks," Aldous says. "She's a sweet little number. Not that you have a shortage of sweet little numbers. Shit, don't tell Bryn I said that. Okay, forget it. I'll be up here at the bar."

Aldous staying for the interview? That's a publicist's job, except that I refused to be chaperoned by publicists. I must really seem off-kilter. "You babysitting?" I ask.

"Nope. Just thought you could use some backup."

Vanessa LeGrande is cute. Or maybe *hot* is a more accurate term. It doesn't matter. I can tell by the way she licks her lips and tosses her hair back that she knows it, and that pretty much ruins the effect. A tattoo of a snake runs up her wrist, and I'd bet our platinum album that she has a tramp stamp. Sure enough, when she reaches into her bag for her digital recorder, peeping up from the top of her low-slung jeans is a small inked arrow pointing south. *Classy.*

"Hey, Adam," Vanessa says, looking at me conspiratorially, like we're old buddies. "Can I just say I'm a huge fan? *Collateral Damage* got me through a devastating breakup senior year of college. So, thank you." She smiles at me.

"Uh, you're welcome."

"And now I'd like to return the favor by writing the best damn profile of Shooting Star ever to hit the page. So how about we get down to brass tacks and blow this thing right out of the water?"

Get down to brass tacks? Do people even understand half the crap that comes spilling out of their mouths? Vanessa may be attempting to be brassy or sassy or trying to win me over with candor or show me how real she is, but whatever it is she's selling, I'm not buying. "Sure," is all I say.

A waiter comes to take our order. Vanessa orders a salad; I order a beer. Vanessa flips through a Moleskine notebook. "I know we're supposed to be talking about *BloodSuckerSunshine* . . ." she begins.

Immediately, I frown. That's *exactly* what we're supposed to be talking about. That's why I'm here. Not to be friends. Not to swap secrets, but because it's part of my job to promote Shooting Star's albums.

Vanessa turns on her siren. "I've been listening to it for weeks, and I'm a fickle, hard-to-please girl." She laughs. In the distance, I hear Aldous clear his throat. I look at him. He's wearing a giant fake smile and giving me a thumbs-up. He looks ludicrous. I turn to Vanessa and force myself to smile back. "But now that your second major-label album is out and your harder sound is, I think we can all agree, established, I'm wanting to write a definitive survey. To chart your evolution from emo-core band to the scions of agita-rock."

Scions of agita-rock? This self-important wankjob deconstructionist crap was something that really threw me in the beginning. As far as I was concerned, I wrote songs: chords and beats and lyrics, verses and bridges and hooks. But then, as we got bigger, people began to dissect the songs, like a frog from biology class until there was nothing left but guts—tiny parts, so much less than the sum.

I roll my eyes slightly, but Vanessa's focused on her notes. "I was listening to some bootlegs of your really early stuff. It's so poppy, almost sweet comparatively. And I've been reading everything ever written about you guys, every blog post, every 'zine article. And almost everyone refers to this so-called Shooting Star "black hole," but no one really ever penetrates it. You have your little indie release; it does well; you were poised for the big leagues, but then this lag. Rumors were that you'd broken up. And then comes *Collateral Damage*. And pow." Vanessa mimes an explosion coming out of her closed fists.

It's a dramatic gesture, but not entirely off base. *Collateral Damage* came out two years ago, and within a month of its release, the single "Animate" had broken onto the national charts and gone viral. We used to joke you couldn't listen to the radio for longer than an hour without hearing it. Then "Bridge" catapulted onto the charts, and soon after the entire album was climbing to the number-one album slot on iTunes, which in turn made every Walmart in the country stock it, and soon it was bumping Lady Gaga off the number-one spot on the *Billboard* charts. For a while it seemed like the album was loaded onto the iPod of every person between the ages of twelve and twenty-four. Within a matter of months, our half-forgotten Oregon band was on the cover of *Time* magazine being touted as "The Millennials' Nirvana."

But none of this is news. It had all been documented, over and over again, ad nauseam, including in *Shuffle*. I'm not sure where Vanessa is going with it.

"You know, everyone seems to attribute the harder sound to the fact that Gus Allen produced *Collateral Damage*."

"Right," I say. "Gus likes to rock."

Vanessa takes a sip of water. I can hear her tongue ring click. "But Gus didn't write those lyrics, which are the foundation for all that oomph. You did. All that raw power and emotion. It's like *Collateral Damage* is the angriest album of the decade."

"And to think, we were going for the happiest."

Vanessa looks up at me, narrows her eyes. "I meant it as a compliment. It was very cathartic for a lot of people, myself included. And that's my point. Everyone knows something went down during your 'black hole.' It's going to come out eventually, so why not control the message? Who does the 'collateral damage' refer to?" she asks, making air quotes. "What happened with you guys? With you?"

Our waiter delivers Vanessa's salad. I order a second beer and don't answer her question. I don't say anything, just keep my eyes cast downward. Because Vanessa's right about one thing. We *do* control the message. In the early days, we got asked this question all the time, but we just kept the answers vague: took a while to find our sound, to write our songs. But now the band's big enough that our publicists issue a list of no-go topics to reporters: Liz and Sarah's relationship, mine and Bryn's, Mike's former drug problems—and the Shooting Star's "black hole." But Vanessa apparently didn't get the memo. I glance over at Aldous for some help, but he's in deep conversation with the bartender. So much for backup.

"The title refers to war," I say. "We've explained that before."

"Right," she says, rolling her eyes. "Because your lyrics are *so* political."

Vanessa stares at me with those big baby blues. This is a reporter's technique: create an awkward silence and wait for your subject to fill it in with babble. It won't work with me, though. I can outstare anyone.

Vanessa's eyes suddenly go cold and hard. She abruptly puts her breezy, flirty personality on the back burner and stares at me with hard ambition. She looks hungry, but it's an improvement because at least she's being herself. "What happened, Adam? I know there's a story there, *the* story of Shooting Star, and I'm going to be the one to tell it. What turned this indie-pop band into a primal rock phenomenon?"

I feel a cold hard fist in my stomach. "Life happened. And it took us a while to write the new stuff—"

"Took *you* a while," Vanessa interrupts. "You wrote both the recent albums."

I just shrug.

"Come on, Adam! *Collateral Damage* is your record. It's a masterpiece. You should be proud of it. And I just know the story behind it, behind your band, is your story, too. A huge shift like this, from collaborative indie quartet to star-driven emotional punk powerhouse—it's all on you. I mean you alone were the one up at the Grammys accepting the award for Best Song. What did that feel like?"

Like shit. "In case you forgot, the whole band won Best New Artist. And that was more than a year ago."

She nods. "Look, I'm not trying to diss anybody or reopen wounds. I'm just trying to understand the shift. In sound. In lyrics. In band dynamics." She gives me a knowing look. "All signs point to you being the catalyst."

"There's no catalyst. We just tinkered with our sound. Happens all the time. Like Dylan going electric. Like Liz Phair going commercial. But people tend to freak out when something diverges from their expectations."

"I just know there's something more to it," Vanessa continues, pushing forward against the table so hard that it shoves into my gut and I have to physically push it back.

"Well, you've obviously got your theory, so don't let the truth get in the way."

Her eyes flash for a quick second and I think I've pissed her off, but then she puts her hands up. Her nails are bitten down. "Actually, you want to know my theory?" she drawls.

Not particularly. "Lay it on me."

"I talked to some people you went to high school with."

I feel my entire body freeze up, soft matter hardening into lead. It takes extreme concentration to lift the glass to my lips and pretend to take a sip.

"I didn't realize that you went to the same high school as Mia Hall," she says lightly. "You know her? The cellist? She's starting to get a lot of buzz in that world. Or whatever the equivalent of buzz is in classical music. Perhaps hum."

The glass shakes in my hand. I have to use my other hand to help lower it to the table to keep from spilling all over myself. *All the people who really know what actually had happened back then aren't talking,* I remind myself. *Rumors, even true ones, are like flames: Stifle the oxygen and they sputter and die.*

"Our high school had a good arts program. It was kind of a breeding ground for musicians," I explain.

"That makes sense," Vanessa says, nodding. "There's a vague rumor that you and Mia were a couple in high school. Which was funny because I'd never read about it anywhere and it certainly seems noteworthy."

An image of Mia flashes before my eyes. Seventeen years old, those dark eyes full of love, intensity, fear, music, sex, magic, grief. Her freezing hands. My own freezing hands, now still grasping the glass of ice water.

"It would be noteworthy if it were true," I say, forcing my voice into an even tone. I take another gulp of water and signal the waiter for another beer. It's my third, the dessert course of my liquid lunch.

"So it's not?" She sounds skeptical.

"Wishful thinking," I reply. "We knew each other casually from school."

"Yeah, I couldn't get anyone who really knew either of you to corroborate it. But then I got a hold of an old yearbook and there's a sweet shot of the two of you. You look pretty coupley. The thing is, there's no name with the photo, just a caption. So unless you know what Mia looks like, you might miss it."

Thank you, Kim Schein: Mia's best friend, yearbook queen, paparazzo. We hadn't wanted that picture used, but Kim had snuck it in by not listing our names with it, just that stupid nickname.

"Groovy and the Geek?" Vanessa asks. "You guys even had a handle."

"You're using high school yearbooks as your source? What next? Wikipedia?"

"You're hardly a reliable source. You said you knew each other 'casually.'"

"Look, the truth is we maybe hooked up for a few weeks, right when those pictures got taken. But, hey, I dated a lot of girls in high school." I give her my best playboy smirk.

"So you haven't seen her since school then?"

"Not since she left for college," I say. That part, at least, is true.

"So how come when I interviewed the rest of your bandmates, they went all no comment when I asked about her?" she asks, eyeing me hard.

Because whatever else has gone wrong with us, we're still loyal. About that. I force myself to speak out loud: "Because there's nothing to tell. I think people like you like the sitcom aspect of, you know, two well-known musicians from the same high school being a couple."

"People like me?" Vanessa asks.

Vultures. Bloodsuckers. Soul-stealers. "Reporters," I say. "You're fond of fairy tales."

"Well, who isn't?" Vanessa says. "Although that woman's life has been anything but a fairy tale. She lost her whole family in a car crash."

Vanessa mock shudders the way you do when you talk about someone's misfortunes that have nothing to do with you, that don't touch you, and never will. I've never hit a woman in my life, but for one minute I want to punch her in the face, give her a taste of the pain she's so casually describing. But I hold it together and she carries on, clueless. "Speaking of fairy tales, are you and Bryn Shraeder having a baby? I keep seeing her in all the tabloids' bump watches."

"No," I reply. "Not that I know of." I'm damn sure Vanessa knows that Bryn is off-limits, but if talking about Bryn's supposed pregnancy will distract her, then I'll do it.

"*Not that you know of*? You're still together, right?"

God, the hunger in her eyes. For all her talk of writing definitive surveys, for all her investigative skills, she's no different from all the other hack journalists and stalker photographers, dying to be the first to deliver a big scoop, either on a birth: *Is It Twins for Adam and Bryn?* Or a death: *Bryn Tells Her Wilde Man: "It's Quits!"* Neither story is true, but some weeks I see both of them on the covers of different gossip rags at the same time.

I think of the house in L.A. that Bryn and I share. Or coinhabit. I can't remember the last time the two of us were there together at the same time for more than a week. She makes two, three films a year, and she just started her own production company. So between shooting and promoting her films and chasing down properties to produce, and me being in the studio and on tour, we seem to be on opposing schedules.

"Yep, Bryn and I are still together," I tell Vanessa. "And she's not pregnant. She's just into those peasant tops these days, so everyone always assumes it's to hide a belly. It's not."

Truth be told, I sometimes wonder if Bryn wears those tops on purpose, to court the bump watch as a way to tempt fate. She *seriously* wants a kid. Even though publicly, Bryn is twenty-four, in reality, she's twenty-eight and she claims her clock is ticking and all that. But I'm twenty-one, and Bryn and I have only been together a year. And I don't care if Bryn says that I have an old soul and have been through a lifetime already. Even if I were forty-one, and Bryn and I had just celebrated twenty years together, I wouldn't want a kid with her.

"Will she be joining you on the tour?"

At the mere mention of the tour, I feel my throat start to close up. The tour is sixty-seven nights long. *Sixty-seven*. I mentally pat for my pill bottle, grow calmer knowing it's there, but am smarter than to sneak one in front of Vanessa.

"Huh?" I ask.

"Is Bryn going to come meet you on the tour at all?"

I imagine Bryn on tour, with her stylists, her Pilates instructors, her latest raw-foods diet. "Maybe."

"How do you like living in Los Angeles?" Vanessa asks. "You don't seem like the SoCal type."

"It's a dry heat," I reply.

"What?"

"Nothing. A joke."

"Oh. Right." Vanessa eyes me skeptically. I no longer read interviews about myself, but when I used to, words like *inscrutable* were often used. And *arrogant*. Is that really how people see me?

Thankfully, our allotted hour is up. She closes her notebook and calls for the check. I catch Aldous's relieved-looking eyes to let him know we're wrapping up.

"It was nice meeting you, Adam," she says.

"Yeah, you too," I lie.

"I gotta say, you're a puzzle." She smiles and her teeth gleam an unnatural white. "But I like puzzles. Like your lyrics, all those grisly images on *Collateral Damage*. And the lyrics on the new record, also very cryptic. You know some critics question whether *Blood-*

SuckerSunshine can match the intensity of *Collateral Damage.* . . ."

I know what's coming. I've heard this before. It's this thing that reporters do. Reference other critics' opinions as a backhanded way to espouse their own. And I know what she's *really* asking, even if she doesn't: *How does it feel that the only worthy thing you ever created came from the worst kind of loss?*

Suddenly, it's all too much. Bryn and the bump watch. Vanessa with my high school yearbook. The idea that nothing's sacred. Everything's fodder. That my life belongs to anyone but me. Sixty-seven nights. *Sixty-seven, sixty-seven.* I push the table hard so that glasses of water and beer go clattering into her lap.

"What the—?"

"This interview's over," I growl.

"I know that. Why are you freaking out on me?"

"Because you're nothing but a vulture! This has fuck all to do with music. It's about picking everything apart."

Vanessa's eyes dance as she fumbles for her recorder. Before she has a chance to turn it back on, I pick it up and slam it against the table, shattering it, and then dump it into a glass of water for good measure. My hand is shaking and my heart is pounding and I feel the beginnings of a panic attack, the kind that makes me sure I'm about to die.

"What did you just do?" Vanessa screams. "I don't have a backup."

"Good."

"How am I supposed to write my article now?"

"You call *that* an article?"

"Yeah. Some of us have to work for a living, you prissy, temperamental ass—"

"Adam!" Aldous is at my side, laying a trio of hundred-dollar bills on the table. "For a new one," he says to Vanessa, before ushering me out of the restaurant and into a taxi. He throws another hundred-dollar bill at the driver after he balks at my lighting up. Aldous reaches into my pocket and grabs my prescription bottle, shakes a tablet into his hand, and says, "Open up," like some bearish mother.

He waits until we're a few blocks from my hotel, until I've sucked down two cigarettes in one continuous inhale and popped another anxiety pill. "What happened back there?"

I tell him. Her questions about the "black hole." Bryn. Mia.

"Don't worry. We can call *Shuffle*. Threaten to pull their exclusive if they don't put a different reporter on the piece. And maybe this gets into the tabloids or Gab-ber for a few days, but it's not much of a story. It'll blow over."

Aldous is saying all this stuff calmly, like, *hey, it's only rock 'n' roll,* but I can read the worry in his eyes.

"I can't, Aldous."

"Don't worry about it. You don't have to. It's just an article. It'll be handled."

"Not just that. I can't do it. Any of it."

Aldous, who I don't think has slept a full night since he toured with Aerosmith, allows himself to look ex-hausted for a few seconds. Then he goes back to man-ager mode. "You've just got pretour burnout. Happens to the best of 'em," he assures me. "Once you get on the road, in front of the crowds, start to feel the love, the adrenaline, the music, you'll be energized. I mean, hell, you'll be fried for sure, but happy-fried. And come November, when this is over, you can go veg out on an island somewhere where nobody knows who you are, where nobody gives a shit about Shooting Star. Or wild Adam Wilde."

November? It's August now. That's three months. And the tour is sixty-seven nights. *Sixty-seven.* I repeat it in my head like a mantra, except it does the opposite of what a mantra's supposed to do. It makes me want to grab fistfuls of my hair and yank.

And how do I tell Aldous, how do I tell any of them, that the music, the adrenaline, *the love*, all the things that mitigate how hard this has become, all of that's gone? All that's left is this vortex. And I'm right on the edge of it.

My entire body is shaking. I'm losing it. A day might be just twenty-four hours but sometimes getting through just one seems as impossible as scaling Everest.

THE INTERNATIONAL BESTSELLER

My name is August.

I won't describe what I look like. Whatever you're thinking,
it's probably worse.

'Has the power to move hearts and change minds' *Guardian*

'Destined to go the way of *The Curious Incident of the Dog
in the Night-Time* and then some' *The Times*

'It wreaks emotional havoc' *Independent*

'Tremendously moving and a novel of all-too-rare power'
Sunday Express

'Incredibly charming, brutal and brilliant' *Observer*